THE DARKLING WOOD
A SCIENTIFIC FANTASY

BRIAN STABLEFORD

WILDSIDE PRESS

For Linda.

I

John Hazard had just started on the pile of first-year essays when there was a rap on the lab door. He didn't get the chance to say, "Come in." Steve Pearlman wasn't the type to wait for an invitation; he was already inside.

Instead, Hazard said, "No. Absolutely not. I told you last time—never again."

"Hi, Doc," Pearlman said, breezily. "Got something here that will interest you." The young man reached into the leather pouch attached to his belt and pulled out a folded map, which he threw on the desk while he rummaged around for something more deeply buried.

Pearlman was in his full ecowarrior regalia: faded blue jeans that probably hadn't been washed for a month, a fawn sweater so thick and lumpy it might have been knitted with chopsticks, and mud-spattered Doc Martens. His blond hair was no longer in dreadlocks, but it looked less tidy than ever.

Steve Pearlman had been Hazard's tutee during the three years he had spent at the university, notionally studying ecology. Hazard hadn't seen a lot of him in the lab or the lecture theatre but had been forced to spend time with him at the beginning and end of every term to discuss the various complaints that invariably accumulated. It had been a great relief to Hazard when Pearlman had actually contrived to get a third-class degree; he hadn't expected to see or hear from him again after the post-graduation piss-up—Pearlman wasn't the kind of student who required his teachers to produce references for dozens of different jobs—but he hadn't been so lucky.

Although Pearlman had never shown overmuch interest in entomology while he'd been studying, the veterans of Crookham Heath had taught him that academics had their uses, and the prospect of the battle of Egypt Mill had sent him scurrying back to his *alma mater* in search of someone prepared to pose an expert on the habits of hawk moths. Hazard was a beetle man, but he'd been so flattered that he'd agreed to appear at the press conference set up to argue that the area between Egypt Mill and Cramborne Barrow ought to be designated a Site of Special Scientific

Interest and that the railway line north of Sutton station ought not to be diverted across it in order to allow the road to be widened.

Unfortunately, the tabloid press had decided to take the other side, and Hazard's name had been an open invitation to pun-hungry headline-mongers. By the time the battle of Egypt Mill was over, ending in victory for "the Establishment" and the bulldozers had actually moved in, Hazard felt as if he'd done a stint on the Somme in 1914. His Head of Department, the venerable Professor Pilkington, and the Dean of the Faculty had been seriously displeased by the damage he'd supposedly done to his department's reputation for objectivity and scientific seriousness. Pilkington had suggested, as tactfully as he was capable of doing so, that Hazard ought to steer clear of environmentalist campaigning in future. Hazard hadn't found that difficult, in conscientious terms, not because he didn't think that the future of the environment was a burning issue of the day, but because he had other things to think about that were far closer to home.

A full thirty seconds had passed by the time Pearlman found what he was searching for in the bottom of his bag. He hauled out a plastic specimen-bottle a little longer and a little thicker than a tube of Smarties, which he passed to Hazard. It was full of small beetles—at least a hundred of them.

The insects had probably been alive when Pearlman had scooped them into the tube, but crowding and lack of air had done for most of them by now. Hazard released the cap in order to provide belated relief for the survivors, but he was careful not to let any escape on to his desk. He fetched a large Petri dish from a cupboard and tipped them into that instead.

The beetles weren't all the same species, but most of them were very similar. Hazard didn't require a magnifying glass to identify the dominant genus, although he suspected that he'd need a microscope to figure out exactly how many species were represented.

"*Tenebrio*, except for three or four undersized carabids and a couple of others," he told his unwanted visitor. "Common as muck. Closely related to my *Tribolium*, except that these aren't specialist grain-beetles—general omnivores, fond of decaying leaves in Autumn, although they won't turn up their noses at fresh vegetable matter, and the adults are perfectly willing to prey on weaker invertebrates, including their own larvae. Thanks to the favors of agriculture, *Tenebrio* species are the most cosmopolitan of all beetles, although most of their immediate cousins prefer a warmer and drier climate. They're farmed in their own right because their larvae are used as fishing bait—mealworms, they're called."

"I knew they weren't woodworm beetles," Pearlman replied, cheerfully. "I wish I could say that you taught me that, but I had plenty of opportunity to get acquainted with that kind of critter when I was at the squat in Curzon Street."

"Some *Tenebrionidae* are wood-borers," Hazard told him, holding the specimen tube up to the light and peering at the interior, trying to find something more interesting than he'd so far seen, "but none of these guys have the jaws for it. Look, Steve, I can't see the point. They're perfectly ordinary species—pests, even—and even if they weren't, they'd be no help to the cause. The hawk moth fiasco must have taught you that no self-respecting tabloid will ever go out on a limb for an insect. Newts maybe—but even that colony of snails on Twyford Down was simply relocated. There's not a single instance on record of a road development being stopped, even at the pie-in-the-sky stage, for the sake of an insect—and this one has to be way past the pie-in-the-sky stage if the Friends have mobilized the Last-Ditch Brigade."

"It's not actually a brigade at present," Pearlman confessed. "Hardly a platoon, so far. Even the Friends don't think this one is worth fighting, but that's because they don't have any domino players on the steering committee. English Nature are prepared to take a stand to defend the relict hedges, but for some reason they don't seem to care that much about pocket-sized patches of woodland. *Tenebrio* are what they call darkling beetles, aren't they?"

Hazard's eyebrows went up in response to the revelation that Steve Pearlman actually knew what a darkling beetle was. "You've already shown these to someone else, haven't you?" he said.

"I can use a library," Pearlman retorted, as he picked up the map again and unfolded it.

It was just a road map, not an ordnance survey map—but that made a sort of sense, given that Steve Pearlman's vocation was trying to make sure that today's road maps didn't go out of date as fast as earlier editions. The makeshift army he'd joined had been so successful back in the nineties, in the wake of the Newbury Bypass War, that no brand new road had been built for a decade within a hundred miles—but that had only served to shift the conflict into a new phase. Road widening was all the rage now that the twenty-first century was under way, and it was very difficult for the protesters to defend sites that already sat alongside significant traffic arteries on the grounds that they were gifted with "Outstanding Natural Beauty" or constituted significant refuges for endangered indigenous wildlife. The tide of public opinion that had briefly got behind the conservationists was dead against them now. It was nearly twenty years since Opération Satanique's sinking of Greenpeace's *Rainbow*

Warrior had helped to fuel a world-scale backlash of resentment against the Juggernaut of Progress, and enviromentalists were nowadays widely considered, at least in South-East England, as defenders of pests, and as pests themselves. Everybody but the Friends of the Earth's "Last-Ditch Brigade" figured that the inevitable cost of not building any new roads was making the most of the ones that already existed.

"There's the new battlefield," said Pearlman, passing Hazard the map.

Hazard looked at the place where the younger man's finger was pointing and frowned. "That's the A303," he said. "I didn't know they had any plans to widen the A303 this year."

"They don't," said Pearlman. "They're widening this one, here."

Hazard had to squint to see it. The "road" that Pearlman was indicating was so small that it didn't even have a B-number. "But it doesn't go anywhere," he said.

"Yes it does," said Pearlman. "It goes to Tenebrion Farm. Tenebrion Farm's in the Domesday Book—I got a friend to check that on line. So far as I can tell, it was a thriving enterprise from the eleventh century all the way through to the nineteenth; then it began to fade, partly because of soil depletion and partly because its owners couldn't or wouldn't fall in with new fashions. It got left behind by the Agricultural Revolution. Its owners tried to catch up in the early twentieth, trying all kinds of supposedly scientific means of fertilization and pest control, but they couldn't restore the fundamental fecundity of the soil and never quite caught up with more efficient and effective competitors. It must have been losing money for generations, save for periods of relief during the world wars and a brief boost when the Common Agricultural Policy gave it a new lease of economic life.

"If the last owner had switched entirely into cereals and rapeseed he might have scraped by, but he didn't. As a penultimate gamble, he built up his dairy herd, just in time to catch BSE and the supermarket price-lock, and the whole operation crashed. He tried a few desperation measures after that—the lunatic even tried switching to potatoes at one stage—but nothing could stem the cash-hemorrhage, and he eventually had to sell up, in a buyer's market. That was when another kind of speculator in, seemingly convinced that housing need in the region had become so urgent that Green Belt regulations would soon be swept away and the eastern edge of Salisbury Plan would become a developers' Klondike. He and all his breed are still waiting, like the Sword of Damocles, for the first few threads of the suspending cord to give way—and this looks like being one of them, unless we can stop it."

"We, in this instance, meaning you and a few of your acolytes?" Hazard suggested.

Steve Pearlman, as a supposed anarchist, did like the term *acolytes*, but he was in full flow and didn't want to pause to argue terminology.

"All the would-be developer could get planning permission to do initially," Pearlman explained, "was revamp the actual farm buildings and their immediate dependencies as a 'modern hamlet,' but there were three big barns as well as a row of workmen's cottages. He's already converted the lot into dwellings, with the encouragement of a local council that had been ordered by Central Government to make provision for 600 extra homes in the next five years. The houses were snapped up in advance of completion and nobody's moved in yet, although the developer and some of his workers have been staying on site, preparing for the final phase, which includes the widening of the road. If that goes ahead, Tenebrion Farm becomes a potential village ripe for expansion. At present, the glorified cart-track connecting it to the A303 isn't even wide enough for two cars to pass one another. That didn't matter while the farmer was driving his tractors back and forth, but the reason the developer built the houses before widening the road was to create what your bog-standard planning application calls *a pressing need for improvement*. It worked—and once the road is widened, the case for building more houses becomes stronger—and so on, one domino at a time."

While Pearlman was talking Hazard had worked out how his ex-student had found out that *Tenebrio* was a darkling beetle. Given his ideological suspicion of computers—although he needed a mobile phone for communication in the field—he had presumably taken the name of the farm to the dictionary and the Britannica in a library. The name of a farm recorded in the Domesday Book couldn't possibly have anything to do with the name assigned to a beetle in the Linnaean classification, but *Tenebrio* was so cosmopolitan that you could probably find specimens on every farm in England if you could be bothered to look. Pearlman had obviously bothered to look—but Hazard still couldn't see what good it was going to do him.

"Well," the entomologist said, carefully, as he put the cap back on the specimen tube and handed it back to the ex-student, "it seems to me that the developer has a good case. Presumably, you're worried about the possibility that once the road is viable, he'll start angling to build more houses either side of it."

"That's how it will begin," Pearlman said. "The real point, though, if you're capable of thinking further ahead, is that the A303 offers an easy connection to the M3. Look to the north, at that cluster of new housing developments west of Hurstbourne Priors. At present, their access roads all connect to the A343, which means that the local yuppies have to make their way over to the M4 in order to head for London, with Newbury sprawling right across their path. The bypass was supposed to make that access easier, of course, but that was more than ten years ago. It's Nightmare Junction now—but once the cart track connecting Tenebrion to the A303 is a real road, the temptation to extend it northwards to give the villagers an alternative way out will become enormous: again, a supposedly urgent need, of the kind that serves as a battering-ram for planning applications.

"The New Tenebrionites won't necessarily like that, of course—all they'll probably want is to be a nice cozy cul-de-sac—but you can bet your pension that the developer always had it in mind. He understands the domino principle, if no one else does. Once he's got the go-ahead to expand his modern hamlet into a modern village he's going to send his bulldozers northwards to plant the spine of a whole bloody town. That's why the battle's worth fighting, and why it's strategically vital to fight it here and now, between the farm and the A-road. The strip to either side of the road's mostly fenced rather than being supplied with hedgerow, like the farmland edging the A303, but there's a little patch of woodland just *here* that must have been there from the very beginning, untouched by the hand of cultivation at least since the Norman invasion, and probably since Roman times. The Domesday Book identifies it as Tenebrion Wood—my bet is that the farm was named after it.

"It's not entirely untouched," Hazard said, raising the specimen tube. "No matter how long Tenebrion Wood's been there, these *Tenebrio* species are invaders, carried into the British Isles with European grains. They might have adapted to local produce, but they're no more native to the wood than you are. I suppose you've considered the argument that setting up tree houses, digging tunnels and getting ready to fight a pitched battle against the developer's so-called security men will completely wreck the fragile ecology of your precious wood, and that even if you did save it from the bulldozers—which you won't—you'd destroy it completely in the process. Anyway, as I already told you, I'm not getting involved. I can't afford the hassle."

"That's what they'll put on the ecosphere's tombstone," Pearlman said, predictably. "*We might have saved it, but we couldn't afford the hassle.* I just want you to take a look, Doc. I just want you to stroll around the site, and tell me whether there's anything better than darkling beetles there—anything we can actually use to start a propaganda war that might get us into the Nationals, or even on TV. It's an exceptional site in more ways than one."

"How, exactly?"

"From the outside it looks like an inextricable tangle, and probably was until the developer got his own surveyor in to make an ecological report, trying to outsmart us before we could get our own campaign off the ground. The surveyor cut a path straight into the heart—convenient for us, in a way, but…well, the thing is that there's a hole in the middle of the wood."

"A clearing, you mean?"

"If you like. I think he already knew it was there—there've been planes taking aerial photographs for the Ordnance Survey department for years, and the gap must have looked odd on the pics. I've been trying to get my hands on some, but even though the Freedom of Information Act came into force years ago, you still have to cut through layers of red tape to get anything out of official channels, even from a backwater like the OS. Anyway, there's a funny hole in the wood, and I can't work out why. You might be able to."

Hazard was an entomologist, not a dendrologist or soil scientist, but he figured that he probably knew enough general biology to make a guess as to why the mysterious clearing hadn't been colonized by the wood, once he had got a look at it…except that he didn't want to look at it.

"What does the developer's report say about it?" he asked.

Pearlman laughed. "As if the developer or his hireling would give us the time of day, let alone useful information!" he said.

"I take it that it wasn't one of my immediate colleagues who carried out the ecosurvey?"

"No, they got someone out from London—Imperial, I think. Name of Nordley. Do you know him?"

"Only by name. He's a plant ecologist."

"Good. That means you might well spot something he didn't, animal-wise. Anyway, the clearing seems to be beetle heaven. I scooped that lot up from Moley's soil-heap in with a single sweep of the tube, before the twilight had completely faded."

"Soil-heap?" Hazard queried. He knew that Moley was the *nom-de-guerre* of one of the "sappers" who had dug tunnels prior to the battle of Egypt Mill. "You've already gone to ground, then?"

"No, it was just a test dig. Moley reckons the clearing's no good for tunneling—the ground's not firm enough. He says he'll try to get down through the tree-roots nearer to the edge of the wood, but it won't be easy. We could really do with digging in, though—the trees are mostly stunted, not exactly the stately oaks of England. Difficult to establish ourselves above head height."

"Not the ideal battleground for stubborn protest, then?"

"Far from it. That's why we need all the clout we can get in publicity terms. We need to make a fuss, mobilize opinion against the Evil Developer. You don't have to lead the charge—just take a look around and give us the benefit of your expertise, in terms of ammunition we can use."

"I've just given you my expert opinion," Hazard told him, flatly—but then he hesitated. "You say you got these from a heap of soil excavated from a dig?"

"Yes. There were a lot more."

"But these aren't burrowers. They can't have come out of the hole."

"Maybe not—if they didn't, the certainly flocked to the stuff that Moley had pulled out, like flies to shit. After food, maybe?"

"They're versatile beetles, but they don't eat soil," Hazard said, contemptuously.

"Maybe soil-heap wasn't the right expression," Pearlman countered. "Looked like rotting vegetable matter to me—you said that's what they like. As I said, it was too soft for tunneling. Organic mud. Humus, if my memory serves me right, is the technical term. Surface, subsoil, substratum and all that crap. "

Obviously, some elements of learning had stuck in the graduate's mind.

"You're exaggerating about the one sweep, though?" Hazard queried. "They're not shy of crowds, but if you got more than a hundred *Tenebrio* in one scoop, there must have been thousands."

"There were," Pearlman confirmed. "They hadn't been there long, though—they must have come rushing from all directions, heading for the stuff Moley had shifted like lemmings off a Norwegian cliff—though not, presumably, to commit suicide."

"That's a myth," Hazard said, reflexively. "Lemmings don't commit mass suicide. That film clip they used to use in anti-smoking ads is a fraud."

Pearlman shrugged his shoulders. He was too young to remember the ad in question. Anti-smoking campaigns had gone through several more phases since then.

"Come and take a look, Doc," he said. "We need you. One day, you know, the front line will reach your back yard, and you'll be screaming for my help."

"My back yard is a cemetery," Hazard told him.

"I know," said Pearlman. "How's that going, by the way?"

Hazard knew that it wasn't a real question—it was just the ex-student's pathetic attempt to reinforce a very tenuous social bond. Even so, his jaw tightened, and he knew that his mouth must be forming a grimace.

Obsessed as he was with his own agenda, the younger man evidently noticed the reaction. "Not well, then?" he said. "Country living not living up to expectations, in spite of living next door to all those lovely insects?"

"None of your business," Hazard snapped, before he could stop himself.

Pearlman's eyebrows raised. "Sorry, Doc," he said. "Didn't know there was a sore spot there, or I'd have been sure not to touch it. Anyway, it doesn't make any difference to the argument. Just because you're living in a redundant vicarage next to a derelict churchyard surrounded by successfully-cultivated fields, it doesn't mean that you're safe in your little Green Belt niche. Take anther look at the map. Even if living next to that folly isn't as much fun as you thought it would be, you won't want to go down the slippery slope that will open if and when they connect your little lane to the A33—and they'll do it. Inch by inch, barn by barn, cart-track by cart-track and wood by wood, they'll worm their way in. Just take a look at my sticking point—that's all I'm asking."

"It's pointless," said Hazard, conscious that his protest sounded weak.

"It's got to be better than marking first-year essays," Pearlman retorted, having cast a rapid glance over the papers heaped on the desk. "It's coming on summertime, and I'll bet you haven't been out in the field since September last, or even spent much time in your beloved churchyard. Now I think about it, you're looking distinctly peaky—not your old buoyant self at all, and the washed-out look only suits the gaunt and the lanky. You've put on weight, haven't you?"

Hazard could have taken offense at that; he was well aware that his lack of height and slightly fuller figure did not lend itself to Byronic depression—although Byron himself had hardly been anorexic, to judge by his portraits. His efforts to slim down and get back to the weight he's had at twenty had, however, been well-and-truly torpedoed by his personal troubles. He knew that comfort eating was unhealthy, but snacking gave him something to do when time and isolation began to weigh on him, as they did far too often nowadays. He suspected that he had put on more than a few pounds since Jenny had left—but he wasn't about to discuss that with Steve Pearlman. All in all, he thought a dignified silence the best response.

"A day out will do you good, Doc, even if you don't find anything," Pearlman persisted. "And who knows? That wood was virgin territory until last week, when Nordley's thugs took a machete to it. I'm sorry you can't be the first person to set foot in it for two thousand years, but surely it's worth a look anyway. You need some fresh air, and it won't cost you anything except time you can spare—I know full well you count your bloody beetles in the mornings, and teaching must have virtually stopped for the exam season. Until the serious marking starts flooding in and you have to get down to pathetic wrangling over exactly which level of meaningless qualification you have to give the cannon fodder, you're your own man. The iceberg's already in sight, Doc, and it's no time to be playing quoits on the deck of the *Titanic*. I know it's a long shot, and that even if you do find something that could help make an argument of sorts for SSI status, it might not do us any good, but we have to try, for fuck's sake. I'm begging you, Doc. Just take a look."

Hazard could feel his resistance melting away. Summer *was* coming on, and he *hadn't* been in the field since the start of the autumn term. In fact, he'd been doing everything on automatic pilot for weeks, stunned by the collapse of his marriage and his life. Even if there was nothing to see in Tenebrion Wood but a stupid clearing and darkling beetles, it would make a change, and a change suddenly didn't seem like such a bad idea.

"Tomorrow's Friday," he said, finally. "In spite of your contempt for the summer term timetable, I'm teaching from two to three, but I can wrap things up for the weekend after that. I can probably reach you by four-thirty, traffic permitting."

"Today would be a lot better," the ecowarrior retorted, unable to suppress a wide grin of self-satisfaction. "The beetles seem to come out in force at dusk. If we go now, you could give me a lift."

As a good Friend of the Earth, Pearlman didn't own a car, but he had no objection to cadging lifts from anyone and everyone.

"Tomorrow," said Hazard, flatly. He figured that he'd made enough compromises for one day, and, perverse as it might seem, he wanted to finish the marking now that he'd started, and get it out of the way.

"I can live with that," said Pearlman, who was apparently prepared to be generous now that he's got what he wanted. "You can leave your car in the lay-by west of the turn-off—it's a good three-quarters of a mile from there to the wood, but the walk will do you good. Bring your wellies—I don't know why it's so muddy, as we haven't had undue quantities of rain recently, but it is. In fact, now I come to think about it, if you insist on making it tomorrow, you can give someone else a lift. I'll tell her to come round to your lab at three, shall I?"

"Who's *her*?" Hazard asked, suspiciously.

"Lady from History—Margaret Dunstable."

Hazard's eyes flicked reflexively to the bookshelf above his desk. "Margaret Dunstable?" he queried, genuinely astonished.

Pearlman misinterpreted the reason for his reaction. "Believe me," he said, "I tried to get someone more respectable, but the entire Archeology department turned me down flat, and I couldn't get a flicker out of anyone else in History, even with the aid of the magic words *Domesday Book*. Anyway, she's not as crazy as she's made out to be."

"She's not crazy at all," Hazard corrected him. "She's probably the sanest person in that entire faculty—which is why they all hate her. But what the hell do you expect her to do for you?"

"God only knows," Pearlman admitted. "But like I say, she was the only volunteer I could find. If you can't find me any rare and arguable precious wildlife, I reckon our best chance is to play the antiquity card. That wood hadn't been touched for two thousand years until the developer send his hired vandals in. If something that old isn't something worth conserving, what is? I wanted a historian to help me play the Domesday Book card—a real historian, not just some twat who spends his time sifting through documents of one or other of the World Wars…someone who knows what a druid was, and cares."

It was on the tip of Hazard's tongue to say that if Pearlman had read Margaret Dunstable's work, he would know that nobody knew what a druid was, and that everything people thought they knew about them was just a tissue of fantasies, but he refrained.

"Okay," he said. "I guess I can do that." It seemed to him, in fact, to be a better reason to take a trip to Tenebrion Wood than looking for exotic insects that he was highly unlikely to find. Margaret Dunstable qualified as rare and precious wildlife in her own right, and even though she and Hazard had been colleagues of a sort for the seven years he'd been at the university, and might even have been in the same room half a dozen times, he had never exchanged two words with her. The Faculties simply didn't mix, except on formal occasions that were extremely unconducive to any authentic meeting and greeting.

"You really don't mind?" said Pearlman. It wasn't really a question; he was just surprised that a hard-headed scientist—even an entomologist—would be willing to let an ancient historian notorious for her scholarly unorthodoxy into his car.

"Not in the least," Hazard assured him. He didn't add any further explanation. He didn't see any necessity to counter the younger man's astonishment with excuses.

"I'll tell her to come at three, then," the eco-warrior repeated. "Thanks. I mean it, Doc—I really do appreciate it."

"Well, Steve, if there's ever anything you can do for me," Hazard said, "I'll be sure to let you know."

II

On Friday afternoon, Hazard hardly had time to put his lecture notes down on his desk and sink into his chair before there was an authoritative rap on the door he'd left ajar behind him. Again he didn't have to shout an invitation to come in, although Margaret Dunstable didn't simply march in the way Steve Pearlman had. She stuck her gray-haired head round the door and said: "Dr. Hazard?" although his name on the door had doubtless informed her that he was unlikely to be anyone else.

"Dr. Dunstable," he said, getting up and going to meet her. Because he'd seen her in the distance in several occasions, he wasn't surprised that she was short and a trifle dumpy, dressed in the quasi-masculine fashion that had probably been standard for female academics back in the 1960s, when there hadn't been very many about. He suspected, though, that Steve Pearlman might have made the same judgment about her that he'd made about Hazard: that her stature would have been more befitting an air of jollity than the slightly haggard sternness that she was trying in vain to combat for the sake of politeness.

He stopped dead when he suddenly realized that the historian wasn't alone. A young woman in her twenties slipped into the lab behind her: slim, blonde, but rather plain of face. The fact that she was dressed in excessively casual clothing and was carrying a pair of green wellington boots didn't help to cultivate an impression of elegance and sophistication. She wasn't exactly radiating *joie de vivre* either, in spite of her youth, but somehow the lack didn't seem as ill-fitting as it did in the older woman.

His surprise must have been evident.

"This is Helen Hearne from Biochemistry," Dr. Dunstable said. "She tells me you've never met."

"Same faculty, different buildings," Hazard muttered. "Sorry, Steve didn't tell me that he'd recruited a biochemist as well. What does he expect you to do for the Cause, Miss Hearne?"

"I'm just a postgrad, not a certified expert," Helen Hearne replied. "I knew Steve slightly when we were undergrads. I wasn't actually a member of Greenpeace or the Friends, but I was a kind of fellow traveler. He was always trying get me to commit. I met him as he was leaving the

Campus yesterday and he picked up the thread of the argument exactly where time and circumstance had broken it—begged me to come and take a look at some goblin wood or other, said he'd already arranged a lift and all I had to do was turn up. He said you wouldn't mind."

"It's fine," Hazard said, reflexively, but frowned anyway. "Why *goblin* wood?"

It was Margaret Dunstable who answered. "That's what the Latin *Tenebrion* and the English *Darkling* originally implied," she said. "They refer to some kind of localized night-spirit, not necessarily malevolent but potentially dangerous."

"Steve Pearlman thinks his precious wood is *haunted*?" said Hazard, incredulously.

Dr. Dunstable smiled. "I doubt it," she said, "but he thinks that the people who named it must have thought that it was. He probably hopes that it might be another lever for possible use in making a media issue out of his defense campaign—and he's probably right. Fantasy is always more newsworthy than dull fact. With all due respect to your specialism, goblins are more likely to catch the public imagination than beetles, even though the beetles have the advantage of actually existing. Is your vehicle in the car park outside?"

While he was processing the observations regarding the previously-unsuspected connotations of the word *Tenebrio*, Hazard reacted to the innocuous addendum. "Twenty paces from the door," he said. "I always arrive early, to get a good spot."

"And to make a start counting your flour-beetles, no doubt," said Dr. Dunstable, still smiling in the same contrived fashion.

That stung a little. Every since Hazard had been a postgrad, people had been making jokes about the supposed incongruity of a man spending his life counting beetles raised on a diet of wholemeal flour, every seventy-two hours for the long term experiments, every twenty-four hours for the shorter runs he carried out at intervals for the purpose of recalibrating the typical generation-span of his populations.

"I hadn't realized that my work was that notorious," he observed, genuinely not meaning it as an item of catty repartee—but Margaret Dunstable probably had an exceptional sensitivity to words like "notorious."

"Unlike mine," she answered, sardonically, taking an inference that he hadn't intended to imply.

Although the two women had already started edging toward the door, Hazard took a couple of steps back into the desk and took Margaret Dunstable's *Scholarly Fantasies in Ancient British History* and its sequel, *Scholarly Fantasies in Medieval History*, off the shelf above it.

He showed them to her. "I'm familiar with your work," he told her, intending to impress her with the fact that he wasn't just aware of her as a comic figure of campus gossip.

She seemed genuinely surprised, presumably because she didn't expect to have many readers in the Biology Department.

"Thank you," she said. Realizing the reason for his gesture, she added: "I didn't mean any disrespect to yours."

Hazard returned the books to the shelf, went to the door and held it open for the two women to precede him. There had been a time, back in his postgrad days, when the campus feminists might have refused on the grounds that opening doors for women was masculinist patronization, but Margaret Dunstable belonged to an earlier era and Helen Hearne to a later one; they went through meekly and then waited, in order to allow him to lead the way down two flights of stairs, along the corridor and across the roadway to the car park. They didn't comment sneeringly on his 99 Mondeo the way Steve Pearlman would have been unable to help doing, even while he accepted a lift in it, but he noticed that they automatically observed a system of precedence, the younger woman getting into the back while Margaret Dunstable took the front passenger seat.

"Do you have a map?" the historian asked, presumably prepared to take on the job of navigator if necessary.

"I know how to find the A303," Hazard assured her, a trifle more curtly than he'd intended.

As they pulled out of the car park, Margaret Dunstable said, presumably for the sake of making conversation: "You've helped Mr. Pearlman out before, I gather?"

Hazard deliberately clamped down on his reflexive sarcasm. "He roped me into his games once before," he said, careful in the rephrasing. "I wasn't much help, I fear. The hawk moths didn't tip the balance in his favor, in spite of my special pleading. I don't expect to find anything that will provide publicity capital this time, but I agreed to take a look because he wouldn't take no for an answer. Do you really think there's any profit to be obtained from the wood's name?"

"I doubt it," the historian replied, "And I'm not entirely sure that I'd want to involve myself with that aspect of the affair, or that it would do Mr. Pearlman's cause any good if I did. I'm speaking as someone who was expelled from the Folklore Society for high treason way back in the seventies."

"Really?" said Hazard.

"Yes—the expulsion, at any rate; the *high treason*'s my description, not theirs."

"You can't have been the only skeptical member they had."

"Of course not; it was a matter of decorum rather than conviction. They had a particular objection to the term *scholarly fantasy*, which they considered particularly defamatory—as many of my colleagues did—and I couldn't really defend myself by saying that it wasn't intended to be pejorative, because I wouldn't have been able to convince myself. Being a scientist rather than a historian, you wouldn't feel the sting, and probably approve of anything that takes the humanities down a peg or two."

"That's not the reason for my interest in your work," Hazard told her. "I'm interested in scholarly fantasies in science—especially biology, obviously, although theoretical physics also seems to me to be a vast web of imaginary constructions, mathematically pretty but hardly having any contact with the material world."

"I'm not qualified to judge," she said, modestly. "But there can't be much scope for scholarly fantasy in entomology, surely? It's presumably a purely descriptive science, requiring scientific standards of exactitude, and the bugs are available for study, unlike the events of history, which have to be reconstructed from faint traces."

"That's broadly true," Hazard admitted, "but insects are by no means immune to scholarly fantasization, as witness all the flim-flam about the supposed hive-minds of social insects, and the pseudo-political rhetoric that represents the reproductive individual of a hive as its queen. There's always a theoretical element as well as a descriptive one in any science, and a historical element too. Paleoentomology is a science built on vague scratches in old rocks—insect chitin does fossilize, after a fashion, but not nearly as well as mollusk shells and reptile bones, so most of what we know, or think we know, about the pre-dinosaurian days when insects might have *ruled the word*, as absurd common parlance would put it, is highly speculative—quintessential scholarly fantasy."

"Some people still say the same about the entire evolutionary story," Helen Hearne put in, evidently referring to American Creationists. "They're intent on clinging on to their own scholarly fantasy until the apocalypse arrives."

"I think they call it *the rapture* nowadays," Hazard said.

"It's only rapturous for the virtuous," the historian supplied. "It's eternal damnation for the likes of us."

"The Fundamentalists don't have any argument worth defending," Hazard said, returning to crusading mode, "but the opposition isn't without sin either. Evolutionary theory is full of scholarly fantasies, and if you think your fellow historians and the Folklore Society are sensitive about anyone pissing on their dogmas, you should see stubborn biologists reacting to anyone who suggests that there might be the slightest imperfection in the Darwinist Credo. The only heretics still considered fair game for persecution nowadays as those who can be stuck with labels like neo-Lamarckian—and yet it's the biologists who complain bitterly about the ideological assaults of Fundamentalism. Both sides would unleash the lions into the arena to tear the opposition to pieces if they could…except, of course, that all the Christian propaganda about slaughter in the Circus Maximus is just another fantasy of history, right? The yellow journalism of the day?"

"Very probably," Margaret Dunstable agreed. Mischievously, she added: "You're planning to write a book on *Scholarly Fantasies in Biology*, then? You're ambitious for pariah status within your community?"

"The idea had crossed my mind," he admitted. "But if you're implying that I'd be too much of a coward, you're probably right. Not everyone has your courage. You don't regret doing it, I assume, even if you did get drummed out of the Folklore Society?"

"Oh, don't mistake me for Edith Piaf," the historian said, making an effort to speak lightly, but conspicuously looking out of her side window at the trees planted along the roadside. "Personally, I regret everything… but that's my age, I suppose, and the effect of circumstances that have nothing to do with history or scholarly fantasy."

Hazard didn't know how to react to that. He had some inkling as to what she probably meant, campus gossip being what it was, but it wasn't conversational territory he wanted to get into. The fact that Margaret Dunstable was making a point of not looking in his direction gave him a pretext for looking behind briefly as he pulled up at a traffic light in order to meet the gaze of his other passenger. Helen Hearne didn't look away.

"I don't suppose there's much scope or scholarly fantasy in bio-chemistry, is there, Miss Hearne."

"Helen," she corrected, reflexively. "I haven't read Dr. Dunstable's books, so I only have a vague idea what you mean, but we're in a data-collecting phase at the moment, with the first phase of the Genome Project only just complete. Ever since Celera got involved, mapping genomes has become routine endeavor, and there's an enormous amount of information to gather, while sophisticated proteonomics is only just getting under way. The number of known organic compounds has increased from a handful to a multitude in the space of a single academic career, and evaluating their properties is a surface that's hardly been scratched, so there's a lot of purely descriptive work to be done. On the other hand, the relentless search for therapeutic applications of newly-synthesized compounds is, if I understand you right, a field chock-full of scholarly fantasies. Even now, medicine is still ninety per cent superstition, so far as I can see. I'm just a chromosome-cruncher, though."

"You're involved in phase two of the HGP?" Hazard asked.

"No—the university doesn't have a slice of that. I've been working on sequencing primitive organisms—bacteria and worms. Haven't even worked my way up to anything as complex as an insect yet. In time, we'll be able to connect up the big picture, but for the moment, thousands of different people are busy just trying to calculate the shapes of the pieces in the puzzle."

"It's a field with a great deal of scope, though," Margaret Dunstable put in. "There's a lot of potential there for future discovery."

"Ancient British history hasn't entirely run out of discoverable data," Hazard felt obliged to point out. "Metal detectors might have been a mixed blessing, but archeologists are making progress hand over fist in excavations all over the country. It's fuel for real discoveries as well as scholarly fantasies."

"I was never much of a digger," Margaret Dunstable admitted. "I was always what the excavators describe, contemptuously, as an *arm-chair historian*."

"I noticed that you didn't bring a pair of wellingtons, like Miss… Helen, that is. Steve must have told you to."

"I don't own a pair," the historian confessed. "Mr. Pearlman said that he has some spare pairs in the camp. But you don't seem to have any either."

"In the boot of the car," said Hazard. "I'm an entomologist—tools of the trade. Not that I've been out in the field much lately. I'm in dire danger of becoming what the contemptuous wing of my field calls a *lab rat*."

"Steve says that you live next door to what he describes as *a real bug-mine*, though?" Helen Hearne put in.

"For a supposedly serious environmentalist, he sometimes has a rather contemptuous turn of phrase himself," Hazard observed. "I live in house that used to be a small vicarage. The church is derelict and the old cemetery that surrounds it is somewhat overgrown with weeds and brambles, but it does play host to a varied population of insects. The remnants of the old village were swallowed up by the surrounding farmland many years ago, but the boundary of the church land still has what English Nature calls relict hedges on the outer edge—centuries-old hedgerows, which form a kind of mini-reserve for birds and insects, and a few small mammals—although there's just a stone wall on the side facing the house. My research is in experimental population dynamics, though—all lab work, not involving any field investigations. As Dr. Dunstable says, I owe my slight notoriety to my semi-continuous culture experiments with flour beetles, which extend over years. Most experiments in population dynamics use bacteria and protozoa, which have generation times measured in hours, but dealing with organisms that have a generation time of thirty days requires longer-term planning."

"But you have assistants and postgrads to help with the counting, I suppose?"

"I wish. It's hardly a sexy field. Grant applications go nowhere. It's rather a sore point in the department, where we're all supposed to be pulling our weight in shopping for research funds. I might yet achieve pariah status even without writing a book on *Scholarly Fantasies in Biology*. The entomology course doesn't actually draw in students now that we've fully instituted a pick-and-mix curriculum. At least you don't have that problem, Dr. Dunstable?"

She didn't raise any objection to the honorific; obviously she wasn't as quick to move on to first name terms as Helen Hearne. It was her turn, however, to say: "I wish. Ancient and Medieval British History is far from being what you call a sexy field, in spite of the fact that the TV news always reports new archeological finds with such avid enthusiasm. The students prefer modern history, and, as you say, the pick-and-mix system makes departmental funding support dependent on the popular courses. When the university can force me to retire, this time next year, there won't be anyone who'll be genuinely sorry to see me go."

Hazard had no difficulty at all in picking up the bitter subtext of that remark. The university probably constituted the whole of Margaret Dunstable's social life as well as her professional life. She had never married, and rumor didn't credit her with any long-term relationship, as it probably would have done if she had one, the sex-lives of lesbians attracting even more prurient interest than those of their heterosexual peers, and Dr. Dunstable having come out way back in the days when there was still a stigma attached to the preference. Many academics looked forward to retirement because they had elaborate plans to settled down to serious writing—which provided an incentive even if the projects turned out to be pipe-dreams—but she probably had no illusions about the ability of that kind of work, on its own, to provide an adequate *raison d'être*.

"I'll be genuinely sorry when you're gone," Hazard told her, not merely as a matter of simple politeness. "The university, and the world, need people prepared to challenge established orthodoxies and play devil's advocate."

"That's not an orthodox conception of need, alas," she said, "and probably not an accurate one, whatever some old fart of a playwright having said about progress depending on unreasonable people. At the end of the day, being unreasonable only attracts opprobrium."

"If you'll forgive me saying so, Dr. Dunstable," Hazard ventured. "You seem a trifle depressed."

"Of course I'm depressed," she retorted. "Anyone who isn't depressed in today's world is insane." She was quick to turn to look at Helen Hearne, though. "Except for the young, of course. The young have no excuse for a lack of hope, and they need the fuel of optimism to keep them going—and biochemistry is a genuinely valuable field of endeavor."

Hazard took note of the fact that she hadn't automatically included him in the category "young," even though he was still in his early thirties, and that she hadn't included entomology in the category of genuinely valuable fields of endeavor—but he couldn't blame her for that. He would have been willing to bet that in a depression contest, he could give her close-run race, in spite of her existential advantages.

He couldn't think of anything else to say, though, and Helen Herne didn't seem inclined to pick up the thread of the conversation, so silence fell for a few moments—a slightly embarrassed silence on all parts.

As a good Englishman, Hazard fell back on the tried and tested. Peering through the windscreen at the solidly gray sky, in which the descending sun was invisible to the west, he observed: "It looks like rain. Not the best afternoon for an excursion. At least we're only a few weeks from the solstice; it won't get dark for hours."

"Is the traffic always this bad?" Helen Hearne put in.

"It's Friday," Hazard observed. "I don't know where all the extra vehicles come from, but Fridays always bring them out of the woodwork. What they used to call rush hour—although pedants really ought to have insisted on crawl hour—starts at three o'clock on Fridays. You don't drive, then?"

"I have a license, but I don't need to," the postgrad replied. "I live within walking distance of the campus, and the economy of not owning a car is a big help when you're living on a grant."

"Even the undergrads seem to regard it as a necessity of life these days," Hazard commented.

"I'm sorry," said Margaret Dunstable, out of the blue.

"For what?" Hazard asked.

"For snapping, earlier. I didn't mean to put a damper on the conversation and switch it over to talking about the weather and the state of the traffic. We're scholars, damn it—we should have more serious matters than that on our minds. According to Mr. Pearlman, we're on our way to do our bit to help save the planet, or at least a tiny bit of it. Even if we all feel that there's really nothing we can do, we ought to give it some thought, oughtn't we? And there is a hint of mystery about his wood, isn't there, apart from its name?"

"I'm not sure if what Steve calls a hole really qualifies as a mystery," Hazard said, perfectly willing to pick up the cue. "Woods do have clearings in them—even natural woods. But the fact that the wood has been untouched for so long, if the claim is true, would make it highly exceptional. With all due respect to English Nature, almost everything we nowadays think of as Nature is actually the product of human activity. The woodlands of England that haven't simply been cleared have still been subject to influence for millennia, long before the Normans started deliberately managing them as hunting-grounds. Even the jungles of the Amazon and New Guinea are shaped in all kinds of ways by the tribes that live there. Hunter-gatherers don't transform their environment as much as agriculturalists, but nowhere that humans live can really qualify as virgin forest…except, according to Steve, Tenebrion Wood, at least until last week. That's really quite remarkable, given that we're in the south of England, not the wilds of Snowdonia or the Scottish Highlands."

"Do you know this Nordley man that the landowner got in to do his pre-emptive ecological survey?" Dr. Dunstable asked.

"I know the name, but I haven't read any of his work, and the necessity of taking a census of my main experiment every seventy-two hours restricts my opportunities to attend conferences and the like, so I've never met him. Steve, obviously, regards him as a lackey of the Enemies of the Earth, but to be honest, if a landowner had come to me to offer me a fee to conduct some kind of ecological survey, I'd have been glad to do it, even if he was a speculator and first cousin to a vulture. It would deflect a little of the criticism from my Department Head with regard to my lack of contribution to the department's image. And I'd probably have taken along a couple of burly students with machetes to clear a path for me, even at the cost of violating the goblin lair. This whole thing is a bit of a farce—not even a game of quoits on the deck of the *Titanic*, as Steve puts it—but you're right to say that the issues behind it are serious, and deserve our earnest thought, even if the world is already past the tipping-point."

"What tipping-point?" asked Helen Hearne.

"The carbon dioxide tipping-point: the amount of greenhouse gas we've pumped into the atmosphere that will make a catastrophic rise in the Earth's surface temperature inevitable."

"But people are talking about deadlines of 2030, or even 2060," the biochemist said. The rise in mean temperature thus far is relatively trivial, even though carbon dioxide levels have increased markedly in the past forty years."

"That's because nobody knows how long the lag phase is between trigger and effect," Hazard said. "The geological time-scale is a relatively leisurely one, because the processes work on such a vast scale, and have all kinds of feedback mechanisms built into them. Statistical models treat the reaction processes as if they were linear, because that's the way stochastic models work, but they're not linear; they're discontinuous, and the present slow increase in global temperature in reaction to the increase in greenhouse gases is like pressure building up in a volcano—nothing much happens for ages, and then there's an eruption. Stabilizing the present level of carbon dioxide in the atmosphere, even if it were politically possible, wouldn't stabilize the atmospheric temperature. There's already enough pollution to produce a catastrophic temperature rise—we just don't know how long it will take to trigger the rapid escalation of that rise. If we're lucky, it might take another twenty years, or even forty, before the explosion—that's practically instantaneous on the geological time-scale—but it's already inevitable. It's a matter now of when the world goes to hell, not if."

"And you think I'm depressed?" Margaret Dunstable commented, as lightly as she could contrive.

"And you think anyone who isn't is insane," Hazard pointed out.

"Touché. It's all right for me, of course—I'm in my mid-sixties. But for you…." This time, she did seem to be including Hazard in the same category as the postgrad, but she didn't bother to spell out the rest of her tokenistic protest.

There was another momentary pause, before Helen Hearne said: "The traffic really is bad, though…but I can't believe it's going to rain." She was joking, but she was the only one who managed a chuckle.

"Well, we're here now," said Hazard, as he made preparations to pull off the A303. "That's the lay-by where Steve told me to park. Not that there's actually room."

The lay-by in question already had three vehicles in it—a Clio, a Citroen Saxo and an Astra—and in order to get the Mondeo off the road Hazard had to make use of a grass verge that wasn't technically part of the lay-by at all, although, in truth, the lay-by wasn't much of a lay-by, more an accidental gap in the verge: a ragged patch of stony ground between the edge of the road and the ugly wire-netting fence bordering a fallow field, where some past farmer had unwisely been sucked into a fad for replacing the hedgerows that most of his neighbors had carefully conserved.

Hazard locked his mobile phone in the glove-compartment before he went to get his wellingtons out of the boot, uncomfortably aware that he had a long and ungainly walk ahead of him.

III

Most of the hedging alongside the road that was scheduled for widening had also been removed in the past, although the fencing erected in their stead had been wooden, so it was slightly less offensive than the wire netting, even though it had long been in dire need of a repair that it was now doomed never to receive. The dearth of intrusive edges made things easier for pedestrians as well as vehicles, though, and it was obvious as they made the left turn that the three of them would have no difficulty keeping out of the way of any vehicles that went past them while they walked along the "glorified cart track." Even though the gate that had once sealed the exit to the A303 had been removed, for the convenience of the new residents of the modern hamlet recently built on the site of Tenebrion Farm, the track still bore a notice saying PRIVATE ROAD: NO RIGHT OF WAY.

It hadn't occurred to Hazard until he saw it that Pearlman's Last-Ditchers would be trespassing, thus requiring him to break the law even to look at the site, but he had come too far to turn around. Cursing himself silently for allowing himself to be sucked in, he began to walk up the narrow lane ahead of his two companions.

The fields beyond the faces to either side hadn't been ploughed or planted for years, but hadn't yet turned back to scrub; the exhausted soil that had probably needed tons of fertilizer to continue producing crops while the agricultural contest was still in full flow was apparently unable to support a rapid return to wilderness, and the bushes and saplings that were trying to grow in them seemed half-hearted, even when they weren't conspicuously sickly. Spring had been warm, but not particularly wet, as spring usually was nowadays, and the grasses that should have been running riot in the fallow fields seemed far from lush. Hazard could see easily enough why the farm had become economically inviable in terms of cereal production, even with the elaborate support of artificial fertilizers.

For the first few hundred yards, during which the track curved gently to the left, there was little or no change in the surroundings. Then Hazard came to the border of Tenebrion Wood—although Pearlman's earlier description of it as "a little patch of woodland" seemed to summarize its limited size and nondescript quality more accurately than the some-what pretentious name. It didn't seem haunted at present—although it was broad daylight, and any surviving night-spirits couldn't really be expected to suggest their presence for several hours yet.

The fences along the track were replaced by the remnants of old hedges as soon the edge of the wood was reached, but the planted haw-thorns were soon replaced by a chaotic mess of thin-boled trees and thick-leaved undergrowth, which crowded together so closely as to make penetration difficult. The foliage loomed over the pathway with dismal effect, although the arching branches hadn't quite contrived to form a tunnel roof. Hazard observed, wryly, that this really was natural wood-land, crammed with sickly and diseased specimens, having nothing of the airy spaciousness of a well-managed and carefully coppiced wood.

It certainly seemed plausible, at first glance, that the site of Tene-brion Wood had never been brought under cultivation, and that it had been let alone, superstitiously, since Roman times, let alone the era of the Norman takeover and the Domesday Book—although, as he'd pointed out to his former student, that was a far cry from being "untouched" in any absolute sense. If Steve Pearlman could scoop up *Tenebrio* beetles by the dozen, Hazard was prepared to bet his last sixpence that other historically-recent invaders would be equally at home here: gray squir-rels, brown rats and black-and-white magpies, as well as hundreds of invertebrate species.

That sort of invasion was not only continuing but accelerating; su-permarket supply chains, cross-channel trains and global warming were now joining forces to import alien species into southeast England on a massive scale. Whatever Pearlman's Last-Ditch Brigade was striving to defend, it wasn't the native ecosystems of Ancient Britain; those were currently in the process of being shot to hell for the fourth or fifth time since the Celts had allegedly imported agriculture to this not-very-green and not-very-pleasant land during the last-little-ice-age-but-one. Except of course, that according to Margaret Dunstable's definitive analysis, "Celts" were just one more scholarly fantasy, invented by armchair an-thropologists.

"It doesn't look like much," observed Helen Hearne, evidently dis-appointed by the sight of the goblin wood.

"That's because it isn't," Hazard said. "Steve certainly can't mount a defense on the ground of Outstanding Natural Beauty." In a spirit of professional scrupulousness, however, he added: "But that doesn't nec-essarily mean that it can't be scientifically interesting."

It wasn't difficult for the three of them to find the gap in the thicket through which access to the wood was possible; numerous feet had trod that way recently. Nor was it difficult, by following the trail, to locate the operative base that Steve Pearlman and his half-dozen friends had set up during the last couple of days, although they were evidently trying to be sufficiently discreet not to reveal the extent and nature of their operation to passing vehicles until they had established a defendable vantage-point.

The fringes of the wood weren't so dense that there was nowhere within spitting distance of the road where sufficient undergrowth could be cleared to pitch a tent, but tents were not the key to a serious occupation. The standard tactics of anti-bulldozer brigades involved perches in treetops and, if possible, underground refuges. The traditional chains and padlocks still had their uses, but endurance required a measure of inaccessibility.

As he approached the Last-Ditchers' base of operation, Hazard could see clearly enough that the canopy squad were having some difficulty getting their arboreal platforms and rope bridges into position, and so far as he could see, the sappers—or, more precisely, the lone digger—had barely started sinking a single shaft. By the time he and his companions came into the base-camp the sentry had whistled a warning, and a mud-caked head had bobbed up out of the shaft in question.

"Oh hi, John!" said the muddy head. "Steve said you were expected." He raised his voice to shout, "OK, boys, he's on our side!" before lowering it again to say, "You remember me, don't you?"

Hazard would never have recognized the face of the boy beneath the mask of mud, but the voice would have been a giveaway even if Pearlman hadn't mentioned his nickname the day before. "Um…Adrian," he said. Hazard assumed that it was because his name was Adrian rather than because he was a digger that his compatriots had initially called the boy Moley, but the nickname had presumably helped shape his destiny within the ragamuffin army. Hazard felt that it might have seemed an intimacy too far for him to use the pseudonym, even though Moley had addressed him by his first name.

"Where's Steve?" he asked.

Moley pulled himself out of the hole, revealing a body that was every bit as filthy as his head. "He's showing the skirt round the clearing. He'll have heard the signal—won't be long."

Hazard knew that the digger's use of the word "skirt" wasn't simply a symptom of thoughtless sexism. In road-protest parlance, "skirt" referred specifically to a female outsider—female ecowarriors never wore skirts. Hazard looked around at his own companions, neither of whom was wearing a skirt, although they too would be assigned to the category, unless Helen Hearne eventually decided to make the commitment for which Steve Pearlman was still optimistically fishing.

"Can you find a pair of wellingtons for Dr. Dunstable?" he asked the muddy boy. In fact, the ground on which they were actually treading wasn't particularly damp thus far, but Hazard could see that the undergrowth in the heart of the wood was so dense and thorny that leg-armor would definitely be required.

"Sure," said Moley. "There should be some in the dump."

"Dump" was short for "equipment dump" rather than "rubbish dump." Ecowarriors were very particular about litter disposal.

The boy found a pair of rubber boots and offered them to the older woman. "A bit big, I'm afraid," he said, "but you won't be able to move fast in there anyway, even with the path cut."

"I take it that the developer doesn't know you're here yet," Hazard observed.

"I'm certain that he does," Moley corrected him. "He's been crashing on his glorified building-site for as long as we've been here. He and the other temporary residents caught on as soon as we arrived, and there's been suspiciously heavy traffic on the path they want to widen, pedestrian as well as vehicular. The phones have doubtless been buzzing while they plan their next move. We're not expecting the opening salvo of blustery threats any time soon, though. Our intelligence says that the contractors aren't scheduled to start work in the road until mid-week— that gives them as well as us plenty of time to make strategic preparations. Say, John, you're a scientist—you know about soil structure. I'm having a hell of a job digging this tunnel. There was never any hope in the clearing—the stuff there's like black treacle—but Steve wanted me to dig a way down anyway. I thought it would be better here, but the texture is still weird. If I ever get down far enough to start digging laterally, I'll probably need more wood to shore it up than the lads up top will use to build platforms. Silly, isn't it, having to import wood to a wood? I'd appreciate it if you could take a look and give us an expert opinion."

"I'm a beetle man," Hazard said, unable to think of anything more foolhardy than taking a look at the walls of a hole that had communicated so much filth to the young man's clothing and face. "I sift leaf-litter when I have to, but everything below the humus is out of my jurisdiction. Sorry."

"Well, there's plenty of dead leaves," Moley replied, unresentfully. "What you'd expect in a wood, I guess. Never seen so many creepy-crawlies are there were in the clearing when it began to get dark, after I'd done the test-drill—plenty to exercise you there, I dare say. I figured out that all woods aren't the same when we were at Egypt Mill, but this baby is seriously yucky."

"That's how things go when they're left to themselves," Hazard said, patronizingly. "If the woodcutters don't keep coming in to clear out the old growth and thin out the saplings, and the peasants don't come to collect the dead wood to fuel their hearths, hardly any of the acorns ever grow into mighty oaks. Mother Nature's a real slut when it comes to housekeeping. As for the creepy-crawlies, every frostless winter we have sets off a new population explosion, in spite of the *fin-de-siècle* explosion in pesticide use—it's just one damn plague after another. *Tenebrio* came to Europe to raid our granaries to begin with, but the genus is as versatile as any other vermin. Rats, people, even cockroaches—you name it and *Tenebrio* will give it a run for its money."

Steve Pearlman had now become visible between the densely packed and crooked tree trunks, so Moley must have figured that he had done his bit for the cause of courtesy. With a casual wave of a black hand he disappeared back into his hole.

The woman with Steve was, indeed, wearing a skirt, but she'd had the sense to bring wellingtons. Her hair was cut short, but not as severely as the general run of Steve's female friends, or even as severely as Margaret Dunstable's. She was older than Helen Hearne—more Hazard's age than Steve's.

"Hi, Doc," said Steve. "Glad you could make it." To his companion he added: "This is the entomologist I mentioned—taught me at uni, or tried: John Hazard. Also Margaret Dunstable, historian, and Helen Hearne, biochemist. Dr. Hazard, Dr. Dunstable, Helen, this is Claire Croly."

Claire Croly was clean enough for Hazard not to mind taking the hand she extended. His slight hesitation was caused by the thought that she might be a reporter. "What pretext did he use to drag you out here?" was the politest way he could think of to ask.

"He says the place gets lively after dark," the woman said, obliquely, as she moved on to greet his companions. "Margaret Dunstable, did Steve say?" she said, to the older woman. "*The* Margaret Dunstable?"

"Probably," the historian admitted. "It depends on the context in which you mean the *the*."

"The *bête noire* of the Folklore Society? The Margaret Dunstable who makes the Pendragonists and the Templars foam at the mouth for insisting on referring to them as *lifestyle fantasists*, and the bases of all their various pretentions as scholarly fantasies?"

"Yes," said the historian, with a sigh that seemed slightly contrived, perhaps because she was actually glad to meet two strangers familiar with her work in little more than an hour. "I'm that one."

"Things probably will get lively soon enough," Hazard observed, picking up on Claire Croly's earlier remark because he was curious to know why she's avoided his question. "But it's not the kind of party you wear your best clothes to—and the gatecrashers sometimes get ugly."

"We're not expecting the opposition to turn up mob-handed yet," Steve Pearlman said, sharply. "Not until Monday, at the earliest—and we won't be doing any partying. We're direly undermanned and already behind schedule. Claire's here for the same reason you are: to look over the site."

"You're a biologist?" Hazard said, looking quizzically into the woman's clear brown eyes.

"Not exactly," she said, wryly. "I'm on the staff of the *Fortean Times*."

Hazard felt as if his face had been slapped. The worst suspicion he'd so far entertained was that she might be from the local rag; the truth seemed considerably worse. He rounded angrily on Steve Pearlman, who was wearing the same infuriating grin that had possessed his face when he'd initially closed the trap on his old tutor. "Damn, it, Steve!" he said. "I can't believe you'd set me up for this! Jesus, it's bad enough being fucked over by the *Sun*. Plastering my name all over the *Fortean Times* will just about kill my career."

"I told you yesterday would be better," Pearlman replied, unrepentantly. "You insisted on double-booking yourself."

"I can assure you that I've no intention of plastering your name anywhere, Dr. Hazard," Claire Croly was quick to add. "Or yours, Dr. Dunstable, without your permission. Your presence here is of no relevance to me. Even if something were to happen—and I see no reason, as yet, to think that it will—I'm perfectly prepared to leave your name out of any report I might make, if that's your wish."

Hazard gulped air as he fought to control an outburst of temper that he knew perfectly well to be unreasonable. He was conscious of overreacting, and had surprised himself by the violence of his response. *My nerves are more highly-strung than I thought*, he said to himself, sternly. *Need to keep a tight rein*. He didn't want to make a worse fool of himself by blustering. His gaze flickered back and forth between Pearlman and the woman. "So I'm an afterthought, am I?" he said, trying his best to synthesize levity, as if it were a joke. "I'll be your last hope, if the Fortean Society can't give you any ammunition to fight with."

"If you'd come when I asked," Pearlman pointed out again, "you'd have been in and out before Claire arrived—or Dr. Dunstable, for that matter. It was short notice, I admit, but still—for you, I took the trouble to collect the beetles. All I offered Claire was a cupful of unease—and the name of the wood, of course. You do realize, don't you, that it wasn't named after the beetles?"

"Of course I do," Hazard said, knowing that it wouldn't sound convincing in spite of the fact that it was the simple truth. He was honest enough not to claim that he'd worked it out for himself. "Dr. Dunstable has told me that it referred originally to some kind of elemental spirit."

"Elemental spirits are a scholarly fantasy," Margaret Dunstable put in, unhelpfully. "An invention of the seventeenth century."

"Unlike goblins, which are an unscholarly fantasy," Hazard observed. "But a sprite by any other name…."

Pearlman, still intellectually fully-charged after his visit to the library, was quick to add: "It's not just that *Tenebrion* with an *n* is Old French for goblin; there's an obsolete English word *tenebrio*, which the dictionary defines as a kind of night-spirit." He had obviously consulted the same reference book as Margaret Dunstable.

"Etymology aside, I still don't appreciate your bringing me out to hunt for ghosts and fairies with a reporter from the *Fortean Times*," Hazard informed him, coldly. "And I can't imagine that Dr. Dunstable likes it either."

He looked at the older woman for support, but she simply shrugged her shoulders.

"Actually," said Pearlman, patiently, "I brought *you* out here to look for insects, and Dr. Dunstable to see a location mentioned in the Domesday Book. I brought *Claire* to hunt for ghosts and fairies. It's called not putting all your eggs in one basket. We are the Last-Ditch Brigade, remember? Even the Friends aren't wholly behind us on this one. Do you know how the circulation of the *Fortean Times* compares with that of *The British Journal of Entomology*—or *New Scientist*, come to that?"

Hazard did know; he had always thought it a sad comment on the times in which he was living. "I shouldn't have come," he said, wearily.

"Yeah," said Steve Pearlman, unsympathetically, "well, you thought that yesterday, and you came anyway. Now you're here, instead of feeling injured for no particular reason, you might as well take a look around, mightn't you? Then you can go back to your ivory tower and your lonely graveyard, protect your reputation as a scrupulous bore, and pray that urban blight won't come marching over your own personal horizon for a few years yet." Now that he had Hazard on site, if not precisely where he wanted him, his ever-fragile diplomacy had gone by the board somewhat.

Hazard clenched his jaw, but decided against striking back. He knew that the young man had a point. He had to be careful not to overreact again, lest it become obvious just how fragile he was at present. On the other hand, he did have to hope that this reporter's promise was worth more than the average. He really could do without a mention in the *Fortean Times*—a mention that one or other of his students was, alas, bound to spot.

"OK," he said, eventually. "Show us what you've got. Give us the tour of this supposedly-mysterious clearing."

Most of what Pearlman had, it transpired, was little more than Hazard had already guessed from his first sight of the little wood. The ecowarrior had elected to defend a little corner of Nature that had already been more than half-choked by Nature's own fecundity. The wood had been unhealthy for centuries. Far from bringing it back from the brink, the recent string of mild winters and benign springs had given a tremendous boost to its parasites. More than three in every five of the standing trees were dying, and the leaf-litter that had accumulated with undue rapidity had begun to rot down with almost tropical alacrity.

Hazard pulled some decaying bark off a dead tree to examine the insects scurrying around underneath. Pearlman had called the wood "beetle heaven" but that had just been a come-on. There were more ants and woodlice in the rotten wood than beetles. Moley had been spot on, however, when he'd described the place as "seriously yucky'. All kinds of tiny organisms were having a high old time in the vicinity, including the mealworms that were the larvae of darkling beetles, but the only message implicit in their unusual activity was that this thousand-year-old stand of trees was doomed, regardless of whether or not bulldozers were allowed to pulverize it in the interests of transforming a farmer's access-track into two lanes of neatly-laid tarmac and a pedestrian pavement.

Hazard did, however, play his part conscientiously. He let Steve Pearlman lead the little caravan of which he was a part through an extremely narrow recently-cleared path to the center of the patch of woodland, where there was indeed a circular clearing some twenty yards in diameter, in which the ground was very flat, covered with a carpet of moss and grass but devoid of saplings, or even serious brambles. And in the middle of the ring, like the bull's-eye of an archery target, there was a hole, with piles of excavated dirt arranged around it in a moderately near semicircle: Moley's "test-drill." The space between the end of the improvised trail and the hole was covered with footprints, which had made a kind of sunken pathway, but most of the surface showed no such indentations.

Hazard stepped on to the surface beside the marked pathway in order to head for the hole in the middle, but paused as his boot sank into the softer ground. For a moment, he though it might keep going, but it only went in to a depth of a few millimeters. He moved back on to the strip that was already compressed and set forth, followed by Margaret Dunstable. The others waited on the edge, watching them.

Hazard could not see any unusual beetle activity on the heaps of humus removed from the hole by Moley, nor did the hole itself—which was about three feet deep and not much wider, seem interesting or inviting. He bent down gingerly and took a clasp-knife out of his trouser-pocket, with which he began to stir the black heap. It was, as Steve Pearlman had suggested, mostly ancient leaf-litter, decayed into a slightly glutinous compost. There were insects within it, adults as well as much more numerous larvae and pupae, but not in unusual numbers, and he couldn't see any unusual species; there were earthworms too, inevitably, and numerous woodlice.

Meanwhile, Margaret Dunstable made her way carefully around the semicircle. She was carrying an archaeologist's trowel, which she must have been carrying in the pocket of her jacket, and she was stirring the dirt with the same care as Hazard. He knew, however, that she wasn't looking for insects.

"Steve thinks that there might have been some kind of structure, doesn't he?" he inferred. "He thinks the reason the trees haven't colonized the space might have something to do with…I don't know, foundations of some sort?"

"There's more hope than thought in it," the historian replied, "but yet—that's why he went to the archeologists first. But if the clearing really has been sealed off for hundreds, or even thousands, of years by the surrounding thicket, it's highly unlikely that the remains if any kind of wooden structure would have prevented the vegetation from taking over, and he could see for himself that there's no trace of stone. He didn't say anything, but I think he might have had vague ideas in his mind about druid altars or something similar—he doesn't know the first thing, even about the myth, of course, let alone the fact that I'm notorious for dismissing all the so-called evidence as so much fantasy. Not that it matters—I can't see any evidence here of anything but vegetable decay. Can you?"

"No," said Hazard. "Which is, in fact, slightly weird. Obviously the ground in the clearing is anomalous in some way, but nothing immediately springs to mind to account for the anomaly."

Helen Hearne came to join them then. She was carrying two of the stoppered tubes of the kind that Pearlman had used to bring Hazard the beetles.

"Steve wants me to take some soil samples," she explained. "I can't imagine what he expects me to find, or even to look for, but I might as well, as I'm here. I can run it through a few elementary tests, and I might even get permission to try a dab or two in the mass spec, although the stuff is probably way too complex to produce anything but confusion."

Hazard sighed. "There's nothing interesting here," he said. "I'd better take a look around the outskirts of the wood, though, so that Steve can't accuse me of not having taken the matter seriously."

Pearlman was waiting to escort him back along trail through the thicket. Once they were back in the part of the wood where a person could at least move around, he showed him two other shallow muddy hollows six or seven feet in diameter.

"There's nothing there now," Pearlman said, but they do come to life after dark—or they did last night and the night before, at any rate, when the moths are flying."

"Are there unusual moths, or unusual quantities?" Hazard asked, suspecting that Pearlman was trying to talk him into spending the night in the wood, or at least waiting until after nightfall before making his way back home—and, he supposed, dropping off Margaret Dunstable and Helen Hearne on the way.

"I'm not really much of a judge of the usual," Pearlman admitted. "But there are a lot. Is it worth collecting some, do you think, in case there are unusual specimens among them? I caught a few, but no hawk months…not that they did the trick last time."

"You do know the wood's dying, don't you?" Hazard said.

"I know that a lot of the trees are sickly," The wood's defender said, a trifle reluctantly, "but it's just a bit overcrowded—except in the clearing, of course. Do you know why the trees don't grow there?"

"I can't say for sure, but there are several possibilities. I suppose you asked Helen to collect soil samples in the hope of discovering some anomaly there, but you do realize that she's unlikely to find anything unless you can tell her exactly what to look for?"

"I was hoping that you might be able to do that. You're the biologist."

"So are you, if your degree certificate can be believed—an ecologist, even. Don't you have a hypothesis to account for the clearing?"

"No, I don't," Steve Pearlman admitted, but didn't add a comment suggesting that his degree really wasn't worth much. He hadn't thrown diplomacy completely to the winds.

"The developer's surveyor probably took samples too," Hazard observed, "and even if he didn't bother, Nordley's a far better ecologist than either or us. He could probably identify the reason for the clearing as soon as he stepped into it."

"Yes, but the Evil Developer's not going to let us or anyone else see his report, are they—certainly not if it contains any information we might be able use against them. These hollows are odd, though, aren't they?" Pearlman's expression showed a certain hopeful interest as Hazard tested the second concavity with his fingertips and then dug the blade of his knife into it.

"I think I can guess what's happened here," Hazard said, hesitantly, "and, on a larger scale, in the clearing. The wood might have been untouched by human hand for centuries but that doesn't mean to say that there haven't been changes. Your so-called hole isn't ancient at all, and the cause of the alteration might be hundreds of yards away, if not miles. Let me take a look at the outer rim of the wood, and the surrounding fields. I don't think the crucial evidence will be visible on the surface, but it's worth a look around before I venture a hypothesis. Given that it's not two hours since I was telling Margaret Dunstable that biology is full of unsuspected scholarly fantasies, I don't want to start fantasizing myself without checking as many facts as I can."

"But you don't think it's anything we can use?" Pearlman said, with a sigh.

"Steve, with the best will in the world, I don't think there's anything at all here you can use. This isn't a battle you can win, and I really don't think it's worth fighting.

"It's always worth fighting," the ecowarrior said, stubbornly. "There's a war on, and it has to be fought, silently if not with publicity. They're not going to get us out of here without a struggle. If all we can do is slow the tide, even just a little bit, that's what we have to do."

"It's pointless," Hazard judged, cursing the sticky mud that was now clinging to his fingertips. He plucked a few fresh leaves from a nearby tree that was still alive, hanging on as stubbornly as the Last Ditch Brigade. The leaves seemed dry and peculiarly autumnal, considering that the saps of spring ought to have been rising lustily within the xylem. If he was correct in his speculation regarding the reason for the hollows, though….

Hazard moved on and Pearlman followed. A host of slender branches drew their tips across Hazard's face, but they didn't get tangled in his hair and they didn't leave scratches. They too seemed oddly limp and effete. It was almost as if the wood knew that it was doomed, and had become listless in the face of adversity.

"Don't worry about the stroking," Pearlman said, in a tone that emphasized just a little too much the fact that he was joking. "The spirit of the wood's just trying to get acquainted. Not many thorns at face height. It'll like you, with you being a biologist and all. It doesn't seem to like me much, even though I've come to help it out. The tips are always catching in my hair."

"You should get it cut occasionally," Hazard suggested. "Anyhow, if trees were capable of forming relationships at all, I expect these would want to keep a polite distance until they'd been properly introduced. They're English, after all. They can't take kindly to having shanties connected by ropy ratlines erected in their canopy."

Pearlman laughed at that, politely—but then he got called away by one of his fellow warriors.

Hazard continued his investigations solo, shoving his way through the seemingly amorous undergrowth with as much delicacy as he could to the edge of the wood and then turning to make his way around it, pausing now and again in order to inspect all kind of chewed and pockmarked leaves.

If nothing else, pottering around the outskirts in Tenebrion Wood gave his spotting skills a thorough and much needed workout. There were *Silvanidae* as well as *Tenebrionidae* left over from the days when cereals had been grown on the adjacent fields, numerous *Rhizophagidae* and, perhaps most interestingly, a couple of *Acanthoceridae* that were a long way from their normal subtropical habitat. There was a slim possibility that they might be the first ones sighted north of Southampton, but who would care?

He took the trouble to collect a few of the more interesting specimens, but even after a further hour of assiduous study he couldn't believe that he'd found anything that might be of the slightest relevance to Pearlman's frail hope of mustering public sympathy behind the wood. The simple truth was that Tenebrion Wood wasn't a Site of Special Scientific Interest. The old cemetery behind Hazard's house was much more interesting, in an objective sense, although it wasn't quite as densely populated with beetle species.

When Hazard eventually found himself, a trifle unexpectedly, on the edge of the wood facing the cluster of almost-complete houses that had replaced the barns of Tenebrion Farm, not far from the road scheduled for widening, he figured that it was time to give up and go home. He was about to make his way across the field to the road when everything changed again. Having caught sight of something tiny and black-and-yellow out of the corner of his eye, he took three paces towards it, and knelt down. He hadn't even stabilized his crouching position when a groan of despair escaped his lips.

For a moment, Hazard wondered whether Pearlman might have set him up, and whether he'd been brought in merely to find something that the ex-ecology student had already found. But that didn't make sense. If Pearlman really had seen and identified what Hazard had just found, he'd have known full well that his petty crusade was futile, and that the technologically-assisted execution of the wood was a mere formality waiting to be recognized.

On the other hand, Hazard thought, even if Pearlman hadn't set him up, he had exposed him to the attention of a reporter from the *Fortean Times*, and made him a hostile witness to the front end of a ghost- and fairy-hunt. He still had some cause for resentment.

He was still crouching over his discovery, letting his thoughts wander, when an unfamiliar voice said: "Dr. Hazard, I presume? I see that you've found the last nail in the goblin wood's coffin."

Hazard turned round as he straightened up, and looked the speaker up and down. He must have come from the direction of the houses, and cut across from the cart-track on seeing him in the field. *But how on earth does he know my name?* Hazard thought.

So far as he knew, Hazard had never seen the man before. He was tall, maybe six feet, with dark hair showing traces of gray. He was reasonably well-dressed—not wearing a suit, but far less casually clad than Hazard—and he was wearing ordinary shoes, not wellingtons.

Hazard remembered, belatedly, that he was trespassing—and the other, whoever he was, know his name. And if the implication of what he'd said could be trusted, he also knew what Hazard had just discovered.

"I'm sorry," Hazard said, tentatively. "Do I know you?"

"We've never met," said the other. "I'm Dennis Nordley. It's my work that Mr. Pearlman has brought you here to double-check. I think you'll find, as I did, that there's no reasonable case for conservation of the wood on the grounds of special scientific interest—quite the reverse, in fact."

"You've notified the ministry?" Hazard says.

"Of course—as I'm obliged by law to do. Do they still have those quaint illustrated notices in police stations? I haven't been in one for some time, I'm afraid."

"And you think I have?" Hazard queried.

Nordley smiled. "I didn't mean to imply any insult," he said.

"Since we've never met," Hazard countered, "how do you know who I am?"

"Apart from the fact that you were bending down and looking distraught, having just discovered the residue of a Colorado beetle infestation on the last survivors of the imported potato plants with which this field was once unwisely sown? I fear, Dr. Hazard, that your arrival here was noted by a member of the security firm that the landowner has hired to defend his interests in the case of trouble with your friend Mr. Pearlman. The firm has confronted Mr. Pearlman before, at Egypt Mill, and their representative kindly brought along their dossier on his activities to what he insists on referring to as 'a council of war,' which is taking place at this moment in one of the houses over there. Among other things, the dossier contains a list of car number plates, all neatly coupled with the owners' names. You're on record, I fear, as a friend of the Friends of the Earth…and of their militant wing, to boot. When our meeting was notified of your presence, I immediately volunteered to come to seek you out and talk to you, given that we're likely to be the sanest men on either side of this stupid conflict."

"The landowner's security firm are spying on me?" Hazard said, hardly able to believe it.

"No, they're spying on Mr. Pearlman—not in any very sophisticated fashion, but with sufficient enthusiasm to draw up a dossier, which they then had to stuff with data of some kind, in order to justify the effort. All rather pointless, in my view—but perhaps fortunate, if you can talk your friend into packing his tents and stealing away, in order to fight the good fight elsewhere, on more favorable terrain."

"I've already told him," Hazard said. "He won't listen. I'll tell him about the Colorado beetle, and make him understand that DEFRA will insist on spraying the wood as well as the field to make sure that the infestation is eradicated, but he'll just want to fight the sprayers as well as the bulldozers. To him, DEFRA is just one more enemy to be opposed. I can explain the necessity of exterminating the pest, but I really don't think he'll take a blind bit of notice."

"Ah," said Nordley, seeming sincere in his disappointment. "And I thought I was having problems trying to talk sense into my lot. The representatives of the security firm insist on seeing it as a war too. They actually seem to be looking forward to a conflict. I came down to the meeting to talk sense—although my report should already have done that—not to be consulted about the tactics of battling environmentalist fanatics, but…you and I really don't belong in the middle of this mess, do we, Dr. Hazard?"

"No, we don't," Hazard agreed, but couldn't resist adding: "And I'm not even getting paid."

"Well, there is that, of course," Nordley agreed. "Consultancies look so good on the CV nowadays, don't they?"

"I wouldn't know," Hazard admitted, through slightly gritted teeth.

"You will," said Nordley, serenely. "This war will run and run, and if both sides are going to continue appealing to the tabloid press for support, making SSIs a crucial element in their armaments of propaganda, we ecologists are going to be in demand."

"I'm not an ecologist—I'm an entomologist."

"Just change your label to environmental entomologist. Words can work wonders. Have you worked out what the clearing is?"

"I think so," Hazard parried. "Have you?"

"I think so too. It used to be a pond, just as the two smaller hollows used to be permanent puddles, but they've dried up. Was that your conclusion too?"

Hazard felt that he was being tested, and felt honor bound to show his mettle. "Yes. At a guess, the pond was probably fed by an underground spring that was diverted, probably not that long ago, or depleted because water was drawn off at another point for irrigation purposes. When the water-supply was cut, the three hollows—the big one as well as the two little ones—filled up with leaf litter, creating a kind of mire or mini-peat-bog in the case of the clearing. The cessation of the flow has altered the substratum of the local ecosystem, and it's probably been struggling with adversity for decades. There might be other complicating factors, but that's probably the bottom line. That would explain why the local fields, which presumably used to obtain a fraction of their irrigation from the spring, are in such poor condition. The farm was probably moderately healthy fifty years ago, maybe thirty, but it hasn't been able to recover from the upheaval yet, and there'd probably be a long lag phase, even if it were let alone, before a healthier thicket is able to replace the one that's rotting as it stands. Is that how you read it?"

Nordley didn't even nod his head. "I can see that you've given it considerable thought," was all that he would say. "In terms of wildlife, though, you'll agree that the wood contains nothing worth fighting for?"

"They're not really fighting for the wood," Hazard told him. "They're fighting for a principle."

Nodley spread his arms wide, in a gesture of helplessness. "There's nothing science can do about that, is there?" he said.

"Not a lot," Hazard agreed.

"Can I at least tell my bunch of fanatics that you and I are in perfect agreement about the absence of any rare or endangered species, and that you'll do your best to make your bunch of fanatics see reason?"

"Fine by me," said Hazard. "You'd better wish me luck, though, because I don't think sanity's going to cut it."

This time Dennis Nordley did condescend to nod his head in sad agreement. "You'll notice," he said, "that I haven't asked you who the two passengers in your car are, or who the Citroen Saxo belongs to. I'm not a spy, and I have no interest in feeding the ridiculous dossier—but you might care to mention to your friends that other people are probably trying to find out who they are even as we speak, and will probably succeed."

Hazard couldn't imagine that any of the three women was going to worry unduly about that, any more than he was himself—and there was a possibility that Claire Croly might actually be quietly pleased to think that mysterious security firms were keeping the agents of the *Fortean Times* under observation. Nevertheless, he kept his face straight as he said: "I'll mention it."

"We'll probably meet again some time," Nordley said, stepping forward to offer Hazard his hand.

Hazard scrupulously wiped his hand on his trousers before accepting it. "My pleasure," he murmured, not entirely sarcastically.

He watched the ecologist head back to Tenebrion Farm, where the "council of war" was doubtless waiting avidly for a report on his improvised embassy. Then he walked back along the road to the point where he had first entered the wood, and went in search of Steve Pearlman and his two passengers.

IV

After summarizing what he had found, skipping lightly over what he had hypothesized with regard to the filled-in pond, Hazard delivered his verdict. "Give it up, Steve. It's hopeless. There's nothing here worth defending even now—quite the contrary, in fact—and by the time the Ministry has sent operatives out to annihilate the Colorado beetle, the whole wood will be irredeemably poisoned."

"Even if it were hopeless," Pearlman told him, predictably, "I couldn't give it up. Come on, Doc—this is the future of the planet we're talking about. We have to slow the developers down until the ideological tide turns, and people finally realize that that they're living though an ecocatstrophe. I'm glad the security firm we fought at Egypt Mill is building dossiers on us and treating the campaign as if it's an all-out war, because it proves that they, at least, are taking us seriously, and think that we're a danger to them. I'm glad, too, that DEFRA are coming into the battle lines, and making it clear exactly where they stand."

"Jesus, Steve, you can't make a stand protecting Colorado beetle! It's one of the most dangerous pests there is. It poses a threat to the nation's mash and chips, for Christ's sake! Do you want to alienate the entire working class?"

"I'm not defending the Colorado beetles. They can spray the field. I'm defending the wood."

"Nobody's going to see a difference—and in all honesty, if the Ministry thinks it's necessary to spray the wood, to make sure that there's no hiding place for the invaders, they're right to do so, and everybody's going to be able to see that they're right. You can't possibly find any PR ammunition capable of trumping that card. Even if you get photographs of eerie night-spirits, or trap a whole bloody family of goblins and stick them in a cage at Whipsnade, you can't make out a case for this wood being a site of special scientific interest. You have my solemn word on that."

"That's not enough for me," said Pearlman. "You can't be a conscientious objector in this war, Doc. If you're not part of the solution, you're part of the problem."

"You don't know how true that is," said Hazard, with a sigh. "I'm sorry, Steve. If you'd paid more attention to my lectures, you'd be able to see how badly you'd misjudged this battleground. I hope you're a better judge of goblins than you are of beetles."

"Aren't you doing to stick round until nightfall?" Pearlman protested, seeming genuinely offended that Hazard wanted to cut and run. He turned to Margaret Dunstable and Helen Hearne, hoping for support, but they had been sufficiently impressed by what Hazard had told them even if Pearlman hadn't.

"I think Dr. Hazard's right about the clearing," the historian said. "It's just a filled-in pond that dried up when the spring feeding it was diverted or interrupted. There's no evidence of any human activity that I can see. I can't help you make out a case for any archeological interest, Mr. Pearlman."

"It all sounds plausible to me too," said the biochemist. "I'll take a look at these samples in the lab, and if I find anything interesting, I'll be sure to let you know, but I really don't see any need to hang around until the middle of the night. With all due respect to Miss Croly and the ancient Romans who presumably named the wood, I can't believe that you're going to see any ghosts or goblins."

"I'll stick round for a while," said the reporter from the *Fortean Times*, loyally. "I've got my own car, though, so I don't have to be involved in any negotiations. If you're going, though, Dr. Dunstable, I'd really like to make an appointment to talk to you some time. We Forteans are supposed to be neutral, after all—we collect damned data without committing any belief to it, and a skeptical viewpoint has its uses, in terms of generating usable copy."

Hazard saw Margaret Dunstable raise her eyes heavenwards, but she didn't refuse. "I'm easy to find," she said. "You can phone the university and ask for me any time you like. I'm there all day every day, unlike some of my colleagues."

Hazard tried, unsuccessfully, to suppress the unkind thought that that was probably because she didn't have anywhere else to be, but at least he didn't voice it.

"Let's go, then," he said—and the three of them began the long walk back to the lay-by. It was after eight but still light.

"Well," said Hazard to Dr. Dunstable, by way of making conversation, "it wasn't a complete waste of time. I got to meet Dennis Nordley, you made a contact at the *Fortean Times*, and we've all attracted spies from a private security firm, who are probably watching us through binoculars right now, wondering who the hell the two of you are."

"It was interesting, in a depressing sort of way," opined Helen Hearne. "And at least we've seen Tenebrion Wood before it was obliterated forever."

"And the traffic will be a lot lighter now," said Hazard. "I can probably get you both home in half an hour—except that I don't know where you live."

"Actually," said Margaret Dunstable, "as it's still light, I wouldn't mind taking a quick look at the church and cemetery you mentioned. There might be more of historical interest there than there was in the wood. Unlike Helen, I never even learned to drive, and it's not often I have the advantage of a lift...if it wouldn't be too inconvenient, that is."

Hazard suspected that it wasn't often that she had the advantage of company in the evenings either, but as there was no possibility of moral danger, he couldn't see any reason for objection. He didn't often have the advantage of company nowadays either, and he was a fan of her work.

"Sure," he said. "It's no trouble at all."

Having compared the addresses that his two passengers gave him with his mental map, he quickly worked out that the shortest loop would be to head for his own house in the first instance so that Margaret Dunstable could carry out her brief reconnaissance mission in the old churchyard, then drop Helen off at her block of flats near the university, and then take the historian home before returning to his own house. Helen had no objection to the detour to the church.

"I'm the official keyholder of the church," Hazard explained to Margaret Dunstable. "Although I own the house, and the grounds of the church have been deconsecrated, there are still rules and restrictions attached to both. There's nothing inside the building, through, and I wouldn't be prepared to guarantee the roof against sudden collapse. The beams are all rotten."

"I'm more interested in the gravestones, to be honest," the historian said.

"They're not very impressive, and terribly corroded and overgrown. It's really not possible to read much of the inscriptions."

"I've been in old graveyards before," the old woman assured him. "I'm familiar with the works of time. It's always good to have a reminder, though, of the fact that things really don't last—that everything will be obliterated sooner than we imagine, including our memorials—and before you accuse me again of being depressed, I actually find that a mildly comforting thought, in its way. It puts things in perspective."

"I guess," said Hazard, uncertainly.

"You, of course, have the fossil record to contemplate, and the scale of evolution, so you must have an even keener sense of the ephemeral nature of earthly things…except, I suppose, that you said something about all that being a scholarly fantasy."

"Not evolution as such, and not the time-scale of its progress," Hazard said. "Nor am I skeptical about the role played by natural selection; given the nature of genetic inheritance, it's a logical inevitability. But there are big gaps, which my colleagues sometimes seem to be deliberately ignoring."

"Such as?"

"Well, I suppose the biggest one is that the story has no beginning. We have no idea how the elements of life as we know it evolved chemically, and how they came together to make such a complicated and intricately interrelated system. Logically, there must have been some kind of evolutionary sequence prior to the simplest cells of which we're currently aware, and it must have been long and complex. Presumably, all those proto-living elements were mopped up once living organisms got to the point of being able to feed in them, but because there's absolutely nothing still available to us, we can't even settle the question as to whether life only evolved once, in a single place, or many times in many places, or where that place or those places might have been, let alone gain any insight into the pattern of the first phase of evolution, prior to the emergence of the bacteria cell. In spite of Haeckel's efforts, the real *urschleim* is still a complete mystery. All the theories people come up with bearing on that problem are, by necessity, scholarly fantasies—hypotheses that can't be tested."

"*Urschleim* is German for 'primordial slime,' right?" said the historian.

"Yes. A hypothesis ventured by Ernst Haeckel. Thomas Henry Huxley thought he's found it at one time, in sludge dredged up from the sea-bed, and named the substance in question *Bathybius haeckelii* in Haeckel's honor, but no sooner had Haeckel incorporated it triumphantly into his textbook than Huxley recanted, having realized that the slime was just a product of the chemical decay of organic debris. Poor Haeckel refused to believe it at first, his reputation and image being on the line, but eventually had to capitulate. A classic example of scholarly fantasy in Biology."

His interlocutor nodded her gray-haired head. "And if the pattern I found in history holds in Biology too, the abandonment will have cast a shadow over the whole area, and no one has dared even to look for *urschleim* since, let alone suggest that they might have found some, even though it's logically necessary that there must have been something of the sort at one time?"

"Exactly," Hazard confirmed.

Margaret Dunstable turned to look at Helen Hearne, probably more to prevent her feeling left out than because she thought that the biochemist might be add anything useful to the argument.

The postgrad shrugged. "Dr. Hazard's right, of course," she said. "Living tissue is amazingly complicated, chemically speaking. It's not just a matter of DNA—DNA is useless without RNA, NAD and a host of other collaborators. Explaining how any one of them arose spontaneously is phenomenally difficult; explaining how they *all* evolved and then came together in the fiendishly completed system in which we now see them operating boggles the mind—which is why most of us don't even think about it. If you want a further example of a gap in evolutionary theory, as it presently stands, there's the problem of the heredity of structure."

"Which is?" the historian queried.

"Well, we now understand exactly how genes code for proteins: how, in combination with RNA, they specify and manufacture all the raw materials that cells use in their functioning—but in terms of the basic stock of genes they have and the proteins they can make, there's very little difference between, say, an ostrich and a whale. We know very little about the way in which one egg-cell produces a whale and the other, employing the same building-blocks, produces an ostrich. Embryologists are making good progress in studying the early differentiation of embryos, but the fundamental nature of the structural blueprint is still very mysterious—all the hypotheses that have so far been proposed are the products of imagination, unprovable as yet. Right, Dr. Hazard?"

"Absolutely," said Hazard. "And if we were to go on to more specific issues, such as the evolution of the structure of the brain and its functions—well, I'm sure you're well aware that ninety per cent of psychology and all of metaphysical philosophy consists of scholarly fantasies."

"The idea had occurred to me," Margaret Dunstable said, dryly. "The wonder is that there are some things we *can* know—and even those, we usually get completely wring before we eventually get them right, and the people with an investment in the wrong ideas always defend them, sometimes to the death, in order to hinder their replacement."

"That's typical too," Hazard agreed, and then made an effort to pull himself together. "We're not exactly cheering one another up, are we? Maybe we sane depressed people shouldn't get together to talk about the awful sanity of our depression. At least we have one happy person to keep us in balance."

He meant it as a compliment, of sorts, but Helen Hearne didn't seem to take it that way. "You mean me?" she said, incredulously.

Hazard realized that he might have put his foot in it. Who could tell what private heartaches the young woman might be hiding, a trifle more efficiently than he was hiding his. "Well, I did," he said, "but perhaps I shouldn't make assumptions…and it's none of my business anyway."

"As Dr. Dunstable so rightly says," the biochemist remarked, in an ambiguously jocular tone, "anyone who isn't depressed in today's world has to be insane. Not, of course, that the people who *are* depressed are necessarily sane."

Hazard decided not to construe that as an insult, as it presumably wasn't meant as one.

They had reached the car. Automatically, they took the same seats as before.

"Are you really going to talk to Claire Croly if she rings you up?" Hazard asked Margaret Dunstable, feeing that a change of topic was definitely in order.

"Why not?" the historian said. "I can understand you not wanting her to mention you in any account she might produce of the darkling wood, because you're a serious scientist with a career and reputation to think of, but I'm just a batty old lesbian that everyone thinks is mad anyway. What do I have to lose?"

"You're a serious scholar who provides an invaluable counterweight to the excesses of the scholarly imagination," Hazard told her. "You're not in the least batty, and the only reason you're sometimes accused of it is because you've got under someone's skin and exposed the weakness of their unjustified convictions."

Margaret Dunstable looked out of the window, without responding even with a tokenistic thank you for the compliment. Hazard had no idea what she was thinking.

"Do you read the *Fortean Times*, Helen?" he asked, in order to change the subject yet again.

"I'd never even heard of the *Fortean Times* until I was introduced to Claire Croly," the biochemist confessed. "I had to ask Steve to explain what it is while she wasn't looking. We scientists can sometimes lead slightly sheltered lives, can't we? Although you seem to be unusually widely-read, Dr. Hazard."

"I'm not exactly well up in Fortean material," Hazard was quick to assure her. "I prefer my scholarly fantasies a little more coherent and a little more plausible."

"She knows how to get in touch with you too," Margaret Dunstable pointed out. "Who do you think she's going to call next time she needs background on an article with a biological angle?"

"I count beetles for a living," Hazard pointed out. "Apart from Steve Pearlman, there's nobody in the world who immediately thinks of me when they want an expert opinion—and I think I might have been struck off his Christmas list, even though it really isn't my fault that the only genuinely interesting beetle I manage to find on his intended battlefield is a pest in dire need of extermination."

"He'll forgive you," Helen Hearne opined.

"I'm not sure that I'll forgive him."

"It's not his fault that you found the Colorado beetles either," Margaret Dunstable pointed out. "And his heart's in the right place, even if his head is suffering from a slight case of porcine disorder. Next time, he might have something worth fighting for and you really might be able to help him."

"I'll cross that bridge when I come to it," Hazard muttered. "Just as long as he keeps my name out of this one."

"He will," said the biochemist. "He knows he might need you again. He's not going to alienate you any more than you're already alienated. As Dr. Dunstable says, his heart is in the right place, and although he is a trifle pig-headed, he's not stupid."

The logic of that argument seemed sound enough. Hazard decided to believe it, at least until further notice.

"If counting beetles for a living seems like such a dead end," Margaret Dunstable asked, "why did you steer yourself into it? You must have had other options—and it must be a trifle inconvenient to be compelled to take measurements every seventy-two hours. It must play hell with family holidays."

Hazard suppressed the reflex that almost made him retort to the last remark in a snappish fashion, and concentrated on the question. "I didn't really steer myself into it," he said. "I just didn't steer out of it. Story of my life, really—always had a tendency to follow the road of least resistance, and always stuck with the *status quo* rather than take a leap into the unknown. I first worked with *Tribolium* beetles in my undergraduate practical project, partly because I knew that it was guaranteed to generate a lot of numbers that would give the write-up substance, whereas a lot of experiments people did would leave them thin on reportage if they didn't actually get a result. Then, having got the groundwork in place, continuing the sequence of experiments seemed to be the natural pitch when I applied for a postgrad slot…and I'm still doing it, years later. It's become a way of life. I'm not sure I could start another from scratch now." *In more contexts than one*, he thought, but didn't say aloud.

"You're only thirty-something, God damn it!" the historian observed. "There's time to think like that when you're my age."

"You might not be entirely sympathetic to the Edith Piaf song," Hazard countered, "but I can't see that you've got that much to regret, professionally. You've written two books that anyone could be proud of, and the fact that they put a lot of people's backs up only proves that what you said was true and needed saying. How many of us will be able to say as much when we're coming up to retirement? Not many."

Again, she didn't thank him. Again, she looked out of the window. She really was in a very downbeat mood.

"I suppose Claire Croly will get something out of her trip even if we didn't," said Helen Hearne, meditatively. "The name of the wood alone, together with its antiquity and the fact that it's been untouched for so long will give her plenty of fuel for an article in an offbeat magazine. It really won't matter whether she really sees or hears anything after dark, will it? Her imagination can fill in the gap. She's actually in the scholarly fantasy business—and has an audience for it. Is there a possibility, do you think, that imaginary elemental spirits might provide a case for saving the wood, where all our science can't even begin?"

"Tenebrions weren't elementals," Margaret Dunstable pointed out, pedantically. "Elemental spirits are a seventeenth-century scholarly invention. Latin spirits had no connection with the Aristotelian elements."

"Sorry," said the biochemist, insincerely. "But she can still get an article out of it, can't she? And she might just be able to start a hare running. Superstition sells better than science."

"Even with a token skeptical viewpoint introduced for balance," Hazard mused, "and the kind of expertise that knows that elemental spirits were seventeenth-century invention. She really might call you on Monday morning, Dr. Dunstable."

"I think you can start calling me Margaret now that you're going to show me your graveyard," the historian said, rather than taking up the possibility that she might get dragged into Claire Croly's article. "Is this it?"

They had indeed pulled into the lane leading to the old church and the refurbished vicarage that Hazard called home. Hazard pulled up in the stony patch of ground between the gate to the vicarage garden and the gate to the churchyard. It was just a rusty wrought-iron gate, not an ornamental lych-gate. Hazard escorted Margaret Dunstable to it, and opened it for her politely, but didn't go in with her.

"I'll just pop into the house," he said. "Take as much time as you like; I'll drive you back home when you're finished."

"You're very kind," said the historian.

Helen Hearne followed Hazard into the house rather than accompanying the older woman into the overgrown churchyard. It was getting late and he was feeling hungry. He didn't have enough provisions in the fridge to offer to make the two of them dinner, but he had an abundant supply of biscuits, and plenty of tea and coffee. Helen Hearne gratefully accepted the offer of a cup of tea. She ran a knowing eye over the kitchen before asking the fatal question.

"Do you live here alone, then?"

"I do now," he said, keeping his voice steady. "It was mainly my wife's idea to move out here—the idea of living in the country had always appealed to her—but the reality didn't measure up to her hopes. She found the place creepy rather than romantic, and the isolation difficult to bear. She left me back in January."

"Oh," said the young woman, suddenly remeasuring the situation. "I'm sorry."

"So am I," Hazard couldn't help saying. "If I seem a trifle depressed and edgy, that's partly why. Time heals, they say, but the wound will be raw for some time yet, I fear."

The postgrad couldn't help getting carried away by her curiosity "Do you have children?" she asked.

"No. I suppose the break-up would have been worse if we had…but if we had, she might not have…well, you can follow the line of argument." He changed the subject, abruptly. "Have you started writing up your PhD?"

"Yes—I'm supposed to be finishing this year. In theory, you still have three years to submit after the first set of three concludes, but there's a lot of pressure nowadays to get it done rather than letting it drift. I'm supposed to get it done by September. It ought to be possible. I've got a mountain of data—it's just a matter of sorting out the good bits and fitting them together into some sort of coherent picture…hopefully not what Dr. Dunstable calls a scholarly fantasy."

"You hadn't met her before today, then?" Hazard said, to keep the conversation going, without intending any hidden implication.

"No, of course not—you didn't think when we turned up at your lab together that we were an item, did you?"

Hazard blushed, because the idea had crossed his mind. "No, of course not," he said.

The biochemist must have glimpsed the blush, because she smiled wryly. "She's not my type," she said, presumably meaning to imply that she wasn't gay, but not wanting to say so too assertively while she was alone in a kitchen eating biscuits with a man whose wife had left him five months before. "You're right about her seeming depressed, though. Retirement must seem like quite a threat to someone in her situation."

"Probably," Hazard agreed. "She must have been something of a star once, when she published the book back in the seventies. Her colleagues might have thought of it as fouling the nest, but the general publicity and the pugnacious tone will have won her acolytes among the students. All in the past now, though."

"Acolytes is a polite way of putting it," Helen Hearne observed.

"Actually, I did just mean it in an intellectual sense," said Hazard. "It wasn't intended as a euphemism. They didn't have a sexual harassment panic back then, but a lesbian academic would still have had to be extremely careful in her dealings with female undergraduates. But we shouldn't really be indulging in that kind of speculative gossip, should we? We're scientists, after all."

"You are. I'm still a genetic sorcerer's apprentice."

"You must be applying for jobs, though, if you've started writing up? Or are you going to hang on in the department, helping out with teaching in the hope that a post will eventually open up for which you'll have first refusal?"

"I'm still procrastinating."

"Well, at least you have a choice. There's actually a commercial sector for you to move into, if you want to do that. You're not stuck in the academic rut."

"True—which means that I actually have to make a decision, on which my future hangs. And there are complicating factors."

Hazard assumed that she meant relationship problems—presumably a boy-friend with his own career to sort out—and maybe other issues too, if she was still an environmentalist fellow traveler. Perhaps she was considering, at least semi-seriously, the possibility of shunning employment altogether in favor of activism.

"There's a lot to weigh up," he conceded, neutrally.

"Not that it matters much if you're right about the ecocatastrophe going nuclear at any moment," she observed.

"You mustn't take too much notice of me," Hazard told her. "As Margaret was careful to say to you earlier, you're young enough still to be hopeful, and can't get by without a measure of optimism. Hanging out with people on the brink of retirement and people deeply sunk into the academic rut probably isn't good for you."

"I was actually hanging out with young and dynamic Steve Pearlman," she pointed out. "You just gave me a lift."

"True," Hazard admitted. "I must try to get over thinking of myself as the center of everything—but it's not easy when that's where your viewpoint is located."

Margaret Dunstable came in then. The sun had set and the twilight was fading.

"How's the graveyard?" Hazard asked, as he handed her a cup of tea freshly-poured from the pot he's filled with that expectation, and the severely-depleted biscuit-tin.

"Probably more interesting from your point of view than mine," the historian said, a trifle wistfully, declining the biscuits. "It's long after my period, of course, but it wouldn't be uninteresting if more artifacts had survived in better condition, precisely because it's prior to the Victorian boom in funerary monuments, which gave familiar cemeteries their typical aspect—not a single date later than 1900. I'm assuming that the village died with the Industrial Revolution, obliterated by changes in farming methods and land tenure?"

"That's right," Hazard confirmed. "The last time there was a parish priest resident here was not long after Victoria came to the throne. Mercifully, I didn't have to do the renovation job—the previous owners did that back in the sixties. They presumably found that the dream of rural living didn't live up to expectations either, because the place had been empty for some years before I bought it—relatively cheaply, all things considered."

"Either?" the historian queried. "You're disenchanted too, then?"

"Not exactly," said Hazard, and concentrated on draining his tea-cup.

Margaret Dunstable looked at Helen Hearne, but the biochemist evidently didn't feel that it would be diplomatic to fill in the blank, and remained silent. The historian didn't press the point, but she did say: "It's a nice house. Plenty of character."

"That's estate-agent-speak for odd," said Hazard. "It is odd—but as you say, the graveyard is more interesting from my viewpoint than yours. There's an interesting paper to be written about the particular ecology of old cemeteries, if not a book, but it wouldn't exactly have commercial potential."

"*Scholarly Fantasies in Biology* probably wouldn't sell much better," Margaret Dunstable opined. "Cemeteries do have a certain charm—and lots of visitors, since ancestor-hunting came into vogue."

"Not this one," Hazard said. "I suspect that most of the inhabitants died with the village, devoid of any significant posterity. A sad thought, isn't it, that living alongside all the ancestors that our contemporaries are busy rooting out, there were countless people whose genetic and material heritage simply came to a dead end. Natural selection in action—but far too arbitrary to lend any substantial support to the scholarly fantasy of the survival of the fittest."

"I thought you approved of Darwinian evolution, as a logical consequence of genetic biochemistry?" said Helen Hearne.

"I do—but Darwin never used the term *survival of the fittest* and never liked it. That aspect of the theory was added by Herbert Spencer. Darwin certainly thought that the unduly sickly and weak were weeded out of populations, but he didn't think that the necessary winners in the game of selection were the big and the tough. He thought that the real advantages, especially as far as the descent of humankind was concerned, came from the extension and elaboration of parental care."

"The survival of the caring?" suggested Margaret Dunstable, skeptically.

"Exactly," said Hazard, firmly. "Just think what a difference it would have made to modern thinking if that had been the catch-phrase that dominated discussion, instead of the other."

Helen Hearne laughed. "It's a nice idea," she said, "but I'm not sure it's any more accurate. The big and the strong we've always selected out by means of bloody warfare, but that doesn't mean that the caring have fared any better in the course of history, does it? If you want to account for human evolution, you'd be better off characterizing it as the survival of the cunning, the treacherous and the hypocritical."

Hazard couldn't help wondering whether the biochemist's relationship problems might be a bit more tangled than he's assumed at first, but it wasn't a topic about which he cared to speculate aloud.

"It's getting dark," he said. "Should I take you home now?"

They agreed, without any evident reluctance, that it would be a good idea to call it a day.

Even on roads devoid of traffic it was a full fifteen-minute drive to the block of flats where the postgrad lived, not far from the campus, and a further ten to Margaret Dunstable's not-dissimilar but slightly more upmarket block. The slowly-descending darkness had its effect, though, and the conversation kept lapsing into silence without anyone feeling any particular urgency about its revivification. By the time goodbyes were said, it had attained formularistic banality.

"We'll doubtless meet again," Hazard said to Margaret Dunstable as he completed the mission by dropping her off. "It might be interesting to discuss the points at which the scholarly fantasies you're interested in and the ones that interest me connect and overlap."

"It might," the historian conceded, without overmuch enthusiasm. "Anyway, it's been an interesting evening—thanks for the lift."

"Any time," said Hazard, knowing that, even though he meant it, it sounded like a vague brush-off.

At least he was in town, and was able to stop off at a fish-and-chip shop on the way back out into the country, to feed the hunger that the biscuits had only been able to postpone.

V

Saturday was Hazard's shopping day. He still followed much the same routine that he and Jenny had adopted when they first moved into their little haven of peace, before Jenny had decided that she was a city girl after all and couldn't stand the isolation. Mercifully, she hadn't yet raised the question of divorce, apparently content to let things drift, perhaps until she could apply on the basis of two years' separation rather than concocting a fanciful case regarding his supposedly unreasonable behavior or fictitious adultery…unless, of course, she eventually changed her mind, and offered some kind of continuing relationship, perhaps on condition that he give up the Old Vicarage and make a fresh start.

Preoccupied by thoughts of that nature, he drove into town again, and stopped at the baker's for fresh bread before going on to Asda and stocking up for the week. He filled up the Mondeo's tank on the way back out, with the solemnity of a quasi-religious ritual.

After eating lunch, he went out into the churchyard, to reassure himself that it really was more deserving of the title of Site of Special Scientific Interest than Steve Pearlman's disgustingly fecund wood. It was man-made, of course, including the hedgerows on the far side, but that wasn't the point at issue; the simple fact was that it was a unique environment: a special habitat with precious few parallels. Scrupulously, he conceded mentally that Tenebrion Wood was probably unique too, in its own unprepossessing fashion, in spite of the seeming banality of its insect population—but he still preferred the particular charm of the churchyard.

As Margaret Dunstable had shrewdly deduced, it had been during the Industrial Revolution and the socially revolution consequent upon it, in the early nineteenth century, that circumstances had prompted the forward-looking landowner on whose estate the village had once stood to modernize his methods. He'd concentrated his declining labor-force in the hamlets on the north side of the estate, and he'd demolished the cottages and outbuildings to the north and west of the church so that he could extend the previously-oblong fields tended by his tenants into greatly elongated rectangles that no longer needed such elaborate labor.

According to the admittedly-skimpy historical research that Hazard had carried out when he bought the old vicarage, the squire in question had been the first man in the county to use a steam traction engine to pull a plough, and one of the consequences of his revolutionary spirit had been that it was perfectly simple for him to plan and carry out the obliteration of an entire village and put the land under cultivation. He'd obviously taken his freethinking ways very seriously, because he'd elected to destroy the village rather than the smaller hamlets, thus isolating the church and rendering it effectively redundant.

The Church Commissioners had obstinately refused to sell their own parcel of land, but they hadn't been able to maintain the living; even though the remaining hamlet-dwellers were perfectly willing to walk across the estate every Sunday, they were no longer numerous enough to constitute a viable flock. The commissioners had closed the church and the cemetery and left the vicarage to rot—until their descendants had eventually taken the long-overdue decision to sell it, with the proviso that its exterior aspect was preserved. Preservation had, of course, been impossible in the long term, time and nature being what they were, but the Church Commissioners had never been noted for their ability to see the obvious.

When he had bought the house, after the original buyers had done the hard work of rendering it habitable by modern standards, Hazard had automatically become the official key-holder of the church, although he had no more than a couple of enquiries a year from tourists wanting to look inside—mostly American Mormons making vain attempts to hunt down scraps of evidence relating to the lives of their remoter ancestors. It was the complete failure of their endeavors that had impelled him to the conviction that the village had vanished genetically as well as physically.

The abandonment of the cemetery more than a hundred years before had allowed the graves to develop their own peculiar mini-ecosystems, in which alien flowers still vied for space with grasses, and the cursory stone markers—sparse in what must have been a predominantly wooden population of memorials, and devoid of Victorian elaboration—now supported extraordinary tapestries of lichen and moss. The flowers attracted butterflies and wild bees, but Hazard's favorite neighbors were the *Lampyridae* that illuminated the cemetery faintly, in their flickering fashion, at dusk and even in the darkest of nights. He liked the moths too, as well the bats that accompanied their flight, and the death-watch beetles that were slowly clicking their way through the timbers of the dead church, but he felt a particular sympathy for the fireflies, blinking out their coded signals to distant mates, in the hope of a response.

Margaret Dunstable was right, he thought, as he sat on ancient stone bench; there was something vaguely comforting about the vistas of imagination opened up by contact with the remote past: the evolutionary past as well as the historical past. The idea that there had once been an era of giant insects comparable to the later age of giant reptiles, was, he knew, a scholarly fantasy, but there had, nevertheless, been a period when the insects had been relatively untroubled by the vertebrate predators that eventually evolved to feed on them, and had supplied the ecosystem's top predators themselves.

The remote ancestors of today's multitudinous beetles had been the grazers that had shaped the evolution of plants, as well as the pollinators whose role had only been partially usurped by birds and cumbersome quadrupeds. It was the latter that had been largely responsible for the evolution of succulent fruits, but the evolution of colored and scented flowers had been entirely due to the early insects, and that relationship had largely determined the subsequent evolution of insects and flowering plants alike. Maybe it could be reckoned the survival of the cunning rather than the survival of the caring, but it was a good story anyway, albeit less melodramatic than the fantasy of the survival of the fittest.

At any rate, Hazard knew that a great deal of the beauty in the world had been adapted to the attraction and tastes of insects, not humans, who were esthetically parasitic on bees and flies in that regard. And Helen Hearne's cynicism notwithstanding, it *was*, in his stubborn opinion, a matter of the survival of the caring: the flowers feeding nectar to the insects and the insects giving invaluable mobility to the plant's seeds—and from that came sweet scents and sweet honey, as well as lovely blooms.

All the beauty in the world, at the end of the day, came down to sexual attraction…but much more of it was due to the sex lives of plants and the sex lives of insects than egocentric humans generally gave them credit for, adding up to a vast and multifaceted picture in which merely human sexual concerns were a trifle marginal. Humans had of course, invented horticulture, which certainly added something to the legacy of beauty, but mostly in the spirit of gilding lilies. They had also invented herbicides and insecticides, which were quite another matter, leaving little scope for the survival of the fittest or the survival of the caring… perhaps, as Helen Hearne had suggested, placing an even heavier bias on the survival of the cunning, the treacherous and the hypocritical….

Hazard was still deeply immersed in his desultory contemplation of the peculiar ecology of the derelict graveyard and its fantasized philosophical implications when a police car pulled up in the lane and a uniformed man got out. Hazard made his way back to the wrought-iron gate, but didn't immediately open it. It was as if some instinct led him to keep a barrier between himself and the representative of what was euphemistically known as law and order.

"Can I help you?" he asked, hoping that the answer might be negative.

"Dr Hazard?" the policeman enquired, for form's sake. "Constable Potts, Sherfield. I'm making enquiries about an incident at Tenebrion Wood last evening. I believe you were there."

Hazard's heart sank.

"I was there for a couple of hours," Hazard admitted. "I suppose I was trespassing, technically speaking, but it's hardly a matter…."

The constable frowned. "A complaint regarding trespass was lodged," he admitted, "but I'm here about a much more serious incident." He paused, obviously thinking that Hazard ought to know what he was talking about.

Hazard assumed that the incident in question must have occurred after he and his two companions had left. "You mean some kind of fight?" he queried, jumping to what seemed to be the natural conclusion. "Between the landowner's security men and the protesters?"

"No, sir," the policeman said. "I'm afraid there was a fatal accident. A young man named Adrian Stimpson was killed when a hole that he was digging collapsed."

There was a moment of shock, when Hazard's mind briefly refused to recognize that "Adrian Stimpson" was Moley, but then the pressure of reality asserted itself. "Oh," he said, finally. "I'm sorry. It must have happened after I left."

"Did you speak to the young man while you were there?" the policeman asked, his words falling with appalling weight on Hazard's stunned consciousness.

"Yes," Hazard said, numbly remembering the seemingly trivial conversation whose ominous quality now stood fully revealed. "He asked me if I knew anything about soil structure. He said that he was having going to have great difficulty shoring up his excavation. He asked me to take a look but I said that I wasn't a soil scientist and couldn't help him. I really couldn't. I'm an entomologist. He knew more about soil than I ever did—he spent days underground during the protests at Crookham Heath and Egypt Mill. What could I have done?"

"It was an accident," the constable said. "No one was at fault, except for the boy. The coroner might call it misadventure, but it was just one of those things. There'll have to be an inquest, I'm afraid, but I doubt that you'll be called to give evidence in person. A statement will probably be sufficient—but your testimony is relevant, and it will need to be recorded."

"Yes," said Hazard, still dazed. "Wasn't there anything they could do? I mean, there were half a dozen people there." *And they had mobile phones*, he added, silently. *My going didn't make any real difference. I'd only have been one more pair of hands.*

"Nothing," said the policeman. "He didn't have a chance to call for help, but they were checking on him at regular intervals. As soon as they became aware of the collapse they started digging, in case there was an air pocket, but he must have asphyxiated very quickly. He was long dead when the fire brigade finally got the body out."

The policeman turned as he spoke, having heard the sound of another vehicle drawing up behind his own. It was a red Citroen Saxo.

"If you could drop into the station at Sherfield some time soon, Dr Hazard," Potts added, studying the new arrival, but evidently not with great interest, "you can make a formal statement there. It shouldn't take long. Monday, if you wouldn't mind."

Hazard deduced that Sherfield police station was closed on Sundays, and that Constable Potts didn't know, as yet, that Claire Croly had been in Tenebrion Wood when the accident actually happened. He didn't feel that it was his responsibility to enlighten him on the latter point "Yes, of course," he said. "I'll come over."

The entomologist stood where he was while the policeman went back to his car, nodding politely to Claire Croly and Steve Pearlman as they both got out of the car. Hazard amended his mistaken deduction; the police must have spoken to both of them already.

Pearlman had changed his clothes within the last couple of hours, and the *Fortean Times* reporter was no longer clad in the skirt she'd been wearing the previous evening. They had both showered recently, presumably separately. Hazard hoped that he knew Pearlman well enough to be reasonably sure that the only reason the woman from the *Fortean Times* was with him was that he'd been desperate for a lift. The ecowarrior didn't own a car, and Hazard's house wasn't on a bus route.

"What did you tell him?" Pearlman wanted to know, nodding his head in the direction of the retreating police car.

"Nothing relevant to you," Hazard assured him. "Just the conversation I had with Moley when I arrived."

"It wasn't us who put him on to you," Pearlman was quick to insist. "If we had, we'd have been sure to say that you weren't there when the collapse happened. That Nordley guy must have given him your name, or the security man who took down your car number. You're not even going to say 'I told you so,' then?"

"I didn't tell you so" Hazard said, dolefully. "I didn't tell Moley so either, although I should have done. Would you have told Moley to fill in the hole and pack up if I *had* advised you to do it in so many words?"

"No," said Pearlman. "We were committed. Moley was committed. We have to make sure, now, that he didn't die for nothing. We're even more determined to defend as much of the wood as possible. We think we still have a chance to save something."

"You bastard!" said Hazard. "You mean you're already thinking of this as a publicity opportunity? You're thinking of it as propagandistic capital?"

He glanced at Claire Croly in an interrogative fashion. She shook her head imperceptibly, to signify that she wasn't in on that particular scheme. Hazard wondered what, in that case, she was doing here—and what, in fact, Steve Pearlman was doing here. He couldn't possibly have come simply to find inquire as to what Hazard had told the police, and Hazard wasn't naïve enough to believe that he had come as a matter of courtesy to inform him of the sad event.

"Look, Doc," Pearlman said, "I understand why you're annoyed with me, I do…but there's a bigger picture here. Yes, I have some responsibility for Moley's death, and I feel bad about it, but this is bigger than Moley, bigger than me and bigger than the Colorado bloody beetle. There's a principle at stake."

Steve Pearlman was too young to remember the days when they'd had posters in post offices identifying Colorado beetle as a significant public enemy, although he might have seen one in a police station. Obviously, if he had, he hadn't taken the message in.

"You really don't understand about the beetles, do you?" Hazard said. "They have to be exterminated. Back in the forties, potatoes were about just about the only significant foodstuff that wasn't on ration. They saw us through the war. If Hitler had had an entomologist on his General Staff who could have advised him to equip the Luftwaffe with jars full of Colorado beetles—plundered by his Japanese allies from occupied China, if his American spies couldn't oblige at source—he might never have had to suffer D-Day. Instead, he stuck to incendiary bombs and generated the spirit of the Blitz. They're going to spray the wood whether you like it or not, Steve, and they really do have to do it. This time, at least, the principle has to yield to practicality. And it really doesn't matter; the wood's already nine parts dead."

"Exactly," said Pearlman, "and we need to know why. We need to find out exactly how it's been poisoned, before we let them finish the job and bury the evidence."

Hazard's first reaction to that assertion was angry despair—but then a thought struck him. "Have you seen Helen Hearne?" he asked. "Has she told you that she found something in those samples you got her to take? Is that why you're suddenly talking about poison?"

"Yes and no," said Pearlman. "I've seen her, but she hadn't made a start on the samples. I've geed her up. She might have something by this evening. You couldn't possibly give her a lift again, could you, when you come out?"

"When *I* come out? Are you out of your mind? I'm not setting foot in your doomed goblin wood again."

"It'll regenerate, if it's given the chance." Pearlman said, stubbornly.

"True—but you can't defend a dead wood on the grounds that it will probably resurrect itself in twenty or thirty years' time. Anyway, that's not the issue any more, and you know it. You got someone killed, Steve. It's time to give it up."

"We all knew the risks, including Moley," Pearlman retorted.

"Oh, sure. You all knew the risk of falling out of a tree when the cherry pickers moved in. Poor Moley probably thought he knew the risk of being caught in a collapse if the JCBs came on site before it was completely clear—and probably thought of it as a heroic risk to run—but what killed him was his inability to cope with the sloppy soil. He was just a boy, Steve! He didn't have a clue what he was doing!"

"Yes he did," said Steve. The determination in his voice was tangible. "And what killed him is right at the heart of our case."

"Oh, shit!" said Hazard, hardly able to believe it. "You're not going to claim that the goblins did it, in revenge for the violation of their sanctuary? That it was some kind of curse?"

Again he glanced at Claire Croly; this time the negative movement of the head was more emphatic.

"Of course not," Pearlman said. "The Fortean aspect is a parallel but unconnected campaign. It's the soil itself, Doc—there's something seriously amiss with the soil. It's not just the collapse—there's something seriously weird about it. You left before dark, in spite of me telling you not to, so you didn't see a thing—but we did, in spite of the distraction of Moley's accident and the flat panic it cased. We saw the beetles again—not just thousands this time, but hundreds of thousands. They weren't around by day, but after dark, they were all over the heaps that Moley had dug out, and all over the hollow you said was a dried up puddle, where you stuck your knife in. I don't know what Helen's chemical analysis is going to turn up, but I do know that the insects are evidence, and you're my entomologist, so you have to bloody well take a look at them—not in the daylight, but after dark. How can you turn me down, when it might be the opportunity of a lifetime, to see something really strange, something new? There might be a paper in it—a genuine *discovery*."

Hazard knew that his former student was fantasizing, desperately, in search of something—anything—that might lend support to his insane determination. He knew, too, that commonplace wisdom alleged that one ought to humor madmen, lest they turn nasty. If Pearlman had been on his own, Hazard, still symbolically secure behind the wrought iron gate of the cemetery, would have sent him packing in spite of all his hysterical insistence—but the madman wasn't alone. He had support.

"I can understand your skepticism, Dr. Hazard," Claire Croly said, "But I was there last night, and I wasn't digging furiously with my hands trying to get down to the boy before he choked to death. I saw the insect activity that Steve is talking about. I'm no expert, obviously, but I can't believe that the way those beetles flocked together was natural. And there were moths, too. Steve said their numbers hadn't been out of the ordinary the night before, but they were there in crowds last night—again, in the clearing and around those peculiar hollows. Tell me, Doctor, what could make insects accumulate like that, in vast numbers, in almost no time at all?"

"Pheromones," said Hazard, automatically.

The expression that came over the reporter's face was one of sudden enlightenment. She knew what pheromones were. Everybody did nowadays, since the cosmetics industry had got hold of the concept and turned it into yet another fantasy of advertising.

"Why would the mud from the holes be producing insect pheromones?" she asked. "And for two different species?"

"It wouldn't," said Hazard—but his own tendency to scholarly fantasy had been stimulated, whether he liked it or not, and he couldn't help a speculation escaping his imagination. "But it's theoretically possible, I suppose, if, for instance, the mire were polluted by some kind of poison. There's been a lot of speculation about pesticide residues working their way down to the water table, although it's hard to find any actual evidence. If the spring feeding the pond and the puddles was close to the surface at that point, as it presumably was, and if it was ferrying some kind of pollutant before it dried up—maybe even the dreaded DDT, since it probably dried up fifty years ago—it's not inconceivable that the products of some delayed reaction or slow breakdown process might mimic insect pheromones....but it's all just speculation, and not very plausible."

"There you go!" said Steve Pearlman, triumphantly, ignoring the qualification regarding the implausibility of the hypothesis. "I knew you could do it Doc! Now you have to come out and see for yourself. Helen will bring more test-tubes—lots more. It *is* a site of special Scientific Interest, if not for the reasons we originally hoped. If we can find your pheromonal mimics...."

"You're letting your imagination run away with you, Steve," said Hazard, although he was guiltily aware of the fact that it wasn't Pearlman's own imagination that was bolting, but the horse he'd just supplied. "It's just idle speculation, and it doesn't change anything anyway. Even endangered hawk-moths look good compared with accidental artificial pheromones. To be honest, Miss Croly—or is it Mrs?—you'd be better off building your story on the forgotten folklore of the night-spirits of Wiltshire."

"It's Miss," Claire Croly told him, answering the question reflexively before going on. "The Fortean Movement isn't the Folklore Society, Dr. Hazard. We're actually much more interested nowadays is cryptozoology and scientific mysteries. We mostly leave ghost-hunting and spirit-dabbling to the established specialists, while we try to work actively as an *avant garde*. Treacherous soil producing fake pheromones would be right up my street. I'll keep your name out of my story if you can help me."

Hazard didn't fail to notice that she hadn't promised to keep his name out of her story if he refused to help her.

"This is crazy," he said.

"The world is a lot crazier than most people think," asserted Claire Croly, as a doctrinaire Fortean would. "Anyway, what have you got to lose? A few hours of a Saturday night? You don't have plans, I presume?"

That stung. No, Hazard didn't have plans. He hadn't had plans for Saturday night for quite some time—but the reporter couldn't know about his circumstances, and evidently didn't mean anything particular by the remark.

"Look," said Hazard, "I really don't like this. I don't like the fact that you're going to try to build Moley's death into some kind of martyrdom. I particularly don't like the fact that you're thinking about splashing the whole sorry incident over the cover of *Fortean Times* and make a paranormal circus of it, even if you're not going to attribute the accident to some kind of curse. What about the poor kid's parents, for Christ's sake? What are they going to make of it? Do you really imagine that you can stop the developer widening the access road by establishing the wood as a Site of Special Pseudoscientific Interest? You're out of your mind, Steve—and you have to leave me out of it now, you hear. No more. Ever."

"You're in it," Steve Pearlman said, ominously. "You were there. He asked you to take a look at the soil, and you refused. You owe it to him."

Hazard had already turned back to Claire Croly, thinking that she was the more reasonable of his adversaries. "Don't you have reservations about this?" he asked. "If you were working for the *News of the World*, I could understand it, but you can't have run completely out of ethics working for *Fortean Times*?" He realized as he said it how desperate that sounded.

"It's not as simple as that," the woman replied. "There really is an enigma here. There's something distinctly odd about that boy's death. You really might be able to help solve a mystery, if you'll just go with the flow."

Hazard shook his head. "You went there looking for something weird," he said, slowly. "You went to spend a night in the dark and deathly wood, and even though you don't believe in goblins any more than Steve or I do, you wanted to find something offbeat, something Fortean. And you've convinced yourself that you have, haven't you? Roman night-spirits don't cut it for you any more—this is the twenty-first century, after all—but you still need your fix of mystery, your fix of fantasy. So you've come to me for a thoroughly modern night-spirit, on the *avant garde*, as you put it. I really don't want to play, Miss Croly. Helen Hearne might be willing, and Margaret Dunstable too, but I have too much to lose in getting involved with the lunatic fringe."

The reporter didn't flinch. "You are playing," she pointed out. "You couldn't help yourself, as soon as you were confronted by the mystery. You might not read the magazine, but you're not immune to the fascination it feeds. You weren't there last night, Dr. Hazard; you left, as soon as you'd found the Colorado beetles—something that satisfied *your* particular spirit of enquiry, and gave you a reason to pack up and go home. But if you'd done as Adrian Stimpson asked…."

"I'd like you both to leave, now," Hazard said, more wearily than angrily. "This conversation isn't going anywhere. I don't think I ever want to see either of you ever again."

"Don't be like that, Doc," Pearlman said, trying the palliative approach now that bluster had failed. "We've got something to show you. It won't take a minute. It's in the boot of the car."

"Fuck off," said Hazard, wishing that he'd never blurted out the word *pheromone*.

"Just take a look," said Pearlman, doggedly. "Afterwards, you can tell us to fuck off, if you want, and we'll go like lambs—but first you have to look. We've come a long way, you know."

Hazard let loose an almighty sigh, but he finally opened the churchyard gate and followed Pearlman when the youth led the way back to the

Citroen. He waited patiently while Claire Croly unlocked the boot and raised the hatch.

Inside, sitting between a toolbox and a petrol can, there was a huge glass jar with a capacity of at least three gallons. It had a narrow neck and a rubber stopper, so it was sealed as tightly as the specimen tube Pearlman had brought to Hazard's office, with much the same result. Most of the insects enclosed in the jar were dead—but that still left thousands, perhaps tens of thousands, that were not yet motionless.

Hazard had no idea how many *Tenebrio* beetles would be required to half-fill a three-gallon jar, but he knew that it was a lot—perhaps a million. He could see, too, that there were more than a few carabids mixed in with this lot, hundreds of woodlice, dozens of wolf-spiders and maybe forty or fifty other insect species—and that was just on the outside of the swarm. He could even see a couple of brightly colored burying-beetles. For the most part, though, the beetles were *Tenebrionidae*, genus *Tenebrio*, in a profusion that had surely never been seen outside a serious mealworm farm.

Now, at last, Hazard had to remind himself of what he hadn't quite admitted to consciousness before. *Tenebrio* was basically a grain beetle, like his own *Tribolium*, a granary pest. It had no business being in a dying wood in any considerable numbers, certainly not in such awful profusion as this—not even a dying wood called Tenebrion Wood, which had a Colorado beetle infestation in the margin that had once marked the edge of a potato-field. The hot weather that was becoming so common in summer, as well as the sequence of mild winters, was causing all kinds of unexpected outbreaks, in spite of the mass insecticide assault that was bringing invertebrate Armageddon to England's green and pleasant land, but global warming wasn't a sufficient scapegoat to explain why Tenebrion Wood was sometimes full of darkling beetles, at least by night. That was odd—damnably odd, in fact. If it wasn't fake pheromones, it had to be something else.

"Twenty minutes, it took me to collect those," said Steve Pearlman. "I wasn't entirely sure that you weren't coming back, so I thought I'd better make adequate provision to get you back. I certainly didn't know Moley was going to die. All I knew was that something was happening that shouldn't be, and maybe couldn't be. It was as if they just came up out of the ground, like oil from a well."

"That's ridiculous," Hazard said.

"Yes, it is," said Pearlman. "Where do you think Moley started to dig the shaft you saw him in? Where else but in one of those funny hollows. He thought because the depression was shallow the mire couldn't be very deep—but he was wrong wasn't he? He hadn't heard your theory about the pond and the water supply that dwindled away. He didn't realize that there might be an actual shaft there, and that the anomalous soil might go all the way down to where the underground spring used to be. If you'd stayed, if you'd taken a look, maybe you could have worked it out and explained it to him. But you didn't. Even though I asked you to, and told you that the action couldn't begin until dusk, you left. Now Moley's dead—but not before the beetles came, Doc. Not before the beetles came"

"Are you saying that you think there's a connection between the beetle influx and Moley's death—that the influx caused the collapse?"

"I don't know," Perlman said. "That's why I need you to investigate, instead of playing Greta Garbo. What's so great about being alone in your poxy graveyard, anyhow?"

"It's out of harm's way," Hazard retorted, tight-lipped. "Unlike Tenerbion Wood. The police must have told you to get the hell out—they weren't going to pay any attention to the trespass complaint before Moley's accident, but they could hardly ignore it afterwards, so now you're there in defiance of a police order."

"What are they going to do?" Pearlman said. "Bring in a riot squad from Newbury? Do they even have a riot squad this side of Reading? And are they going to charge through that wood with their riot shields, to drive us out? It's not a crime scene, so the trespass is basically a civil matter. Believe me, Doc, you don't have to be scared of truncheons and tear gas."

"What I'm afraid of," Hazard reminded him, wearily, "is being caught *in flagrate delicto* breaking the law. Even a trivial offence like trespass could be enough to get me the sack, if Pilkington gets to hear about it. You remember Professor Pilkington?"

Pearlman presumably did remember the old fossil in question, but didn't think him worthy of an acknowledgement of acquaintance. "It'll be after dark on a Saturday night in June," he said, instead. "You think the police don't have better things to do to a Saturday night but send people out to the middle of nowhere to see whether a bunch of protesters have moved on? Nobody's going to arrest you, or even see you. Wear a balaclava if you want to preserve your incognito—I'm presuming that you don't own a ski-mask. You really do need to take a look—you'll never forgive yourself if you don't. It's a genuine biological mystery. How many of those do you think you're going to run across in your lifetime, given that you're just a lab rat?"

"You're quite mad, you know," said Hazard.

"The only way you'll be able to say that with authority," Pearlman retorted, "is to come and figure out the sane explanation, if you can. Until then, you can't say for sure where sanity ends and madness begins." He pointed to the jar of invertebrates. "Is that *normal*?"

"No," Hazard admitted, honesty getting the better of him. "It has to be natural, somehow, but it's not normal."

Hazard realized that Steve Pearlman knew how to push his buttons, how to overcome his reluctance, and was prepared to use any method to get him to do what he wanted. If evolution really was a matter of the survival of the cunning, the treacherous and the hypocritical, Pearlman, despite his unprepossessing appearance, was no loser in the game of natural selection. And his heart was, after all, in the right place. One day, the bulldozers really would put in an appearance on his own doorstep—and when that day came, Hazard would be screaming for help from the Friends of the Earth, English Nature, Greenpeace, *Fortean Times* and anyone else who would condescend to listen. If that day came, he knew, he'd be perfectly prepared to populate his private cemetery with imaginary ghosts, and pretend that the empty church had once played host to the Holy Grail: anything to hold back the tide. Tenebrion Wood wasn't his back yard, and the people whose back yard it was wanted it gone, but that wasn't really the point.

"I'm not going out to bat in the pages of *Fortean Times*," Hazard insisted. "Whatever you talk me into seeing, I'm not putting my head on the public chopping block within reach of Pilkington's censorious arm. Not for the Angel of Death with a flaming sword, let alone a night-spirit that takes the form of an uncanny horde of beetles."

"Whatever you see will be for your eyes only, Doc," said Steve Pearlman. "The three of us, plus Helen Hearne. I'll send all the others away for the night—we have to lay in all the necessary provisions before Monday anyway. Don't worry about the security clowns taking down your number plate again—nobody's going to be prepared to give them double pay for anything they could meaningfully do tonight."

Hazard gave in. "What time do you want me?" he asked tiredly.

"If you arrive about ten you should be in good time for the show. You'll have to leave a bit early to pick Helen up, though; factor that into your planning. You'll be though before midnight, I guarantee, unless you find something that makes you want to stay."

"Okay," said Hazard.

Pearlman couldn't resist relishing his victory just a little. "I'll be sure to let the wood-spirit know," he said. "It might not like me as much as it likes you, but good news is always welcome."

"You're mad," Hazard repeated, determined to have the last word, at least for the time being. Pearlman had won enough to give it to him.

Claire Croly shut the boot, and then the two of them got into the car and drove away.

Hazard went indoors; he had had enough of the churchyard for one day.

VI

The thin Saturday night traffic enabled Hazard to get to Helen Hearne's block five minutes ahead of schedule. He was already regretting bitterly having given in to Steve Pearlman's pressure, and was feeling distinctly edgy. He missed Jenny even more at the weekends than on weekday evenings, and all his complex resentments were seething within him, like lava ready to erupt. He pressed the buzzer on the intercom, and she answered instantly, evidently having been waiting for him.

"Wait there, Dr. Hazard," she said. "We'll be right down."

She had switched off before he had a chance to react to the "we."

His curiosity was not of long duration. The biochemist appeared within less than a minute, with Margaret Dunstable on her heels.

Hazard stared at them, letting his surprise and curiosity show.

"Still not an item," Helen Hearne assured him. "When Steve told me about that poor boy I phoned Margaret to let her know the bad news. I told her that I was going back tonight and that Steve had promised to get you to give me a lift. She wanted to come along. You don't mind, I assume? I'd have phoned you if I thought I needed to check."

"Not in the least," Hazard assured her.

When they were in the car, however—in the same formation as before—Hazard turned to the historian and said: "We're a long way from your field now. Steve and his Fortean accomplice are playing it as a combination of scientific mystery and guilt trip—they reckon I owe it to both Moley and myself not to let his death go unexamined. They caught me in their carefully-cast net, and struggling only caused the toils to tighten. What's your excuse?"

"I saw the beginning," Margaret Dunstable said, "and I'd like to see the end. Simple curiosity. Also, I hadn't got anything better to do."

"Well, we can all say that," said Hazard, his bitterness with regard to that particular issue. Before he could stop himself, his tongue bolted yet again with another half-formed thought, and he added: "Anyway, you might score. I think Claire Croly bats for your side."

The historian must have heard way too many sly digs about her sexuality to take serious offence, although she did see a trifle surprised by the impoliteness. "Don't be ridiculous," she said. "For one thing, I can spot a team-mate when I see one, and for another, she'd hardly be likely to fancy an old wreck like me if she were the gayest woman in Wiltshire. You've got more chance than I have, in spite of your lack of charm and the off-putting radiance of self-pity." It seemed that Hazard was not the only one with a touch of the more toxic kind of Saturday night fever.

"Wow," said Hazard. "You don't pull your counter-punches, do you?"

"Training of a lifetime," she said. "Anyway, we're on first name terms now, aren't we? We can have what anthropologists call a joking relationship, whereby we automatically construe apparent insults as innocent quips. It *was* an innocent quip you were trying to make, in your gauche fashion, wasn't it?"

"It was," Hazard confirmed, "and I apologize for the gaucherie—and the lack of charm. The 'radiance of self-pity' was a bit harsh, though."

"Do you want me to ask Helen to serve as referee?"

"On reflection," Hazard said, "no." He glanced in the overhead mirror as he spoke. The postgrad seemed more astonished than amused. She wasn't fully acclimatized as yet to the occasional acidity of academic wit.

Margaret Dunstable turned her head to look at the younger woman. "It's all right, dear," she said. "We're just breaking the ice. We're not strangers any more; we can begin to be friends."

"With friends like that…," the biochemist remarked, joining in the new game.

"On a more serious note," Hazard said, "did you find anything in your test tubes?"

"I can't exactly pop the stuff into the departmental mass spec and press a button," the biochemist replied. "Anyway, that's only magic in TV forensic science programs. If your sample is too complicated, all you get is a mess. I've barely had time to do more that look at the stuff under a good microscope, but it certainly looks odd. Swarming with bacteria, although you'd expect that. Surprisingly soupy, more colloidal than solid. Considering that I took the samples from near the surface, the leaf-litter seemed to have rotted down a long way, but I hesitate to say that some unknown agent had actually dissolved or digested the stiff."

"Why *digested*?"

"The samples have a very low pH—much more acidic that soils usually are. That's probably why new growth can't make much headway there. If there was some pollution of the water supply before the spring dried up, it might be something simpler than a pesticide residues. No formicary smell, but a whiff of vinegar, so probably some acetic acid, and hydrochloric as well. Nordley didn't mention his chemical findings to you?"

"No, although I can't imagine that he'd neglect something as simple as pH measurement. His report is theoretically confidential, though—he probably only told me his pond hypothesis because he was pretty sure I'd already made the same guess, and wanted to appear generous in order to get me on side. Perhaps he already has the data that would explain the sudden collapse of Moley's excavation. It's difficult to believe that it had anything to do with the arrival of the beetles, though. Did Steve show you his three-gallon jar?"

"Yes—he must really have worked hard on that collection. It shows how much he wanted you to come back, Dr. Hazard."

"I feel *so* privileged," Hazard replied.

"You should," Margaret Dunstable observed. "They cut me loose. I'm having to push my way back in."

"You should have spun them a line about a neolithic burial site, or druidic human sacrifices. They'd have been all over you, no matter what you might think about Claire Croly's straightness."

"Don't harp on, dear boy. You can't imagine how tedious vulgar cattiness becomes by the time you're in your sixties, even if you contrived to lived most of your life before Gay Pride made us such an ostentatious *community*. And it really doesn't suit you. Just keep remembering that I'm old enough to be your mother."

"Sorry," Hazard said, again, thinking that what he really needed to remember was the old woman's tendency to sharp overreaction. "That one really was innocuous, though."

"Very much so. You seem to have a talent for it. No wonder your wife left you—no, hang on, that one just slipped out. My turn to say sorry."

"It's okay," Hazard say. "Joking relationship, remember." He couldn't help casting a slightly resentful glance in the mirror, though, figuring that Helen Hearne must have repeated what he'd told her the previous night while the historian was in the churchyard. The biochemist didn't meet his reflected gaze.

"Perhaps we should make this a regular date," Hazard suggested, "since none of us has anything better to do with our Saturday nights."

Nobody reacted to that suggestion, sarcastically or otherwise.

"Well," said Helen Hearne, "it didn't rain yesterday in spite of appearances. Maybe we'll be lucky again tonight."

"I should think so," said Hazard. "There are gaps in the cloud. With luck, we might even get some moonlight, although lovely Phoebe's only half full. Or do I mean that dark Hecate's only half black?"

"If you weren't far too conscientious to drink and drive, Dr. Hazard," Margaret Dunstable opined, "I'd suspect that you'd been on the whisky."

"Haven't touched a drop," Hazard assured her. "And it's John now, remember."

"You're wound up somehow. You really are feeling guilty about not taking a closer look at the soil when the boy asked you to, aren't you?—and deeply resentful of Mr. Pearlman exploiting the fact."

Hazard shrugged his shoulders rather than making a sarcastic reply.

"It wasn't your fault," said the historian, in perfect earnest. "You really shouldn't feel bad about it."

"He was just a kid," muttered Hazard. "I'd have reason to hate myself if I didn't feel bad about it."

The woman who was old enough to be his mother didn't seem to have any difficult suppressing the remark about self-pity that must have been on the tip of her tongue.

"Well, ease up anyway," she said, instead. "You're responsible for our safety as well as your own while you're behind that wheel. I'm worn out, but Helen might yet be a future Nobel Prize winner."

"Provided that she avoids bad company," murmured Hazard.

Even from the back seat, she heard him. "Do you mean Steve," she asked, "or the two of you?"

"There you are," said Margaret Dunstable to Hazard. "Now she's joining in."

"You did call her Helen," Hazard pointed out. "And let's face it, I'm not the only one who's a trifle wound up. We're all on edge—and why not? We're heading for a haunted wood at dead of night, after all, where Moley's ghost might be waiting to curse us for letting him die."

That joke fell flat too.

"This was once a Roman Road, right?" Hazard observed, as he turned on to the A303.

"Fosse Way," Margaret Dunstable supplied, obligingly.

"For the legions marching along it," Hazard went on. "Tenebrion Wood must have been a visible landmark, like Stonehenge. Sometimes, they must have had to camp overnight nearby. Whether the surrounding area was under cultivation or not, it was probably a hunting ground for owls—about which the Romans were very superstitious, if that's not another scholarly fantasy. If the owls perched in the trees routinely, or nested in them…they could easily have become night-spirits, no?"

"And that's exactly how scholarly fantasies are born," the historian said. "A plausible story, based entirely on conjecture. It might even be true…but we can never know."

"Alternatively, of course," Hazard suggested, "the wood might really have been haunted, by some kind of entity that has since become extinct, leading us, in the absence of any evidence in metal or stone, to think that it never existed, as a mere product of the unfettered imagination. There must be entities of that sort—countless biological species that made no impression at all on the fossil record, because they were entirely soft-bodied. Maybe the Romans were more apt than they knew in calling spirits larvae…or biologists more apt than they knew in borrowing the term. Phases in a metamorphic process whose beginning an end we can hardly imagine…."

"Very poetic," said Margaret Dunstable. "Is that where our multitudinous beetles came from, do you think? They were the metamorphic product of larvae in Helen's vinegar-spiced soup?"

"I told you that biology was very amenable to scholarly fantasies," Hazard reminded her. "And practically by definition, they're sexier than fantasies about Roman legionaries mistaking owls for birds of ill-omen. But pedantically speaking, larvae don't metamorphose directly into beetles; they have to pupate first"

"You really ought to write that book, you know, even if it does put you at risk of ending up like me."

This time, Hazard succeeded in suppressing the joke that sprung unbidden to his mind like some kind of mischievous imp. He pulled into the lay-by. There was plenty of space tonight, its only other occupant being Claire Croly's Saxo.

Hazard checked his watch. "Eighteen minutes to ten," he said, "without ever exceeding the speed limit…well, hardly ever. We should make the camp with four minutes to spare, even walking in rubber boots."

"I'll have to borrow a pair again when we get there," Margaret Dunstable remarked. "But that means I won't slow you down in the interim."

Hazard's chronological estimate seemed sound enough as they marched along the lane at a steady pace while the last of the twilight faded away. Lovely Phoebe was only peeping through the clouds at rare intervals, but Hazard had taken the precaution of changing the battery in his flashlight before setting forth, and had pocketed a spare just in case. Unlike Jenny, he wasn't in the least afraid of the dark, but he didn't have a cat's eyes and was just as likely as any common-or-garden coward to get himself filthy or hurt while blundering blindly around. He held the torch ready for action as soon as they reached the gap in the hedge that gave access to the wood.

A few stars were visible amid the clouds, but the light pollution from distant Newbury collaborated with the usual oxides and micro-particles to impart a curious salmon-pink stain to the strip of sky visible above the lane. The remaining patches of hedgerow seemed taller and closer by night than they had by day, and the impression was enhanced by a background susurrus that owed more to the stirring of slender branches in the breeze than to the movement of rodents and birds. Hazard heard an owl hoot once, but it didn't come from the direction of the wood, whose branches were nowadays far too densely packed to allow fliers to perch therein with any degree of comfort, let alone to hunt there.

It was just as easy to find the way to the Last-Ditchers' campsite by night as it had been by day—easier, given the number of booted feet that had tramped back and forth since Adrian's accident and Dr. Nordley's report of the presence of Colorado beetle on the wood's further fringe. As Hazard moved away from the lane he played his light over the ground expectantly, but the only beetles he saw were glossy carabids out hunting. The beam reflected back more than once from tiny pairs of eyes, but they were only hedgehogs.

The track the three of them was following was now a well-worn path, and there was no need for Hazard to fight his way through tangled branches. A few trailing tips brushed his arms, but he was wearing a protective tracksuit top over his T-shirt and there didn't seem to be anything intimate in the way the leaves slid across its synthetic surface.

Steve Pearlman and Claire Croly were waiting for them at the equipment dump. They had torches of their own, but they'd turned them down low in order to conserve power. They seemed surprised to see Margaret Dunstable, but not displeased. Hazard switched his own light off when he joined them, knowing that his eyes were already half-adjusted to the gloom. By the light of Pearlman's torch he could see where the hole that Adrian Stimpson had dug had been filled in again, leaving a convex mound like an oversized molehill. Hazard knew that one always took more dirt out of a hole than was required to fill it again; it was a matter of compaction.

"Well?" said Hazard.

"It feels strange," Pearlman said, looking around to signify that he meant the whole ambience rather than the heap of dirt marking the spite of the disaster.

"That's why I'm here," Hazard said. "It's supposed to feel strange. Goblins to the right of us, kobolds to the left...."

"It's not like that," Claire Croly said. "It wasn't like that last night—but it wasn't like this either. Something's changed."

"Sure," said Hazard. "You're down half a dozen ecowarriors—one of whom is lying in a mortuary—and you're up one skeptic, who can't feel a damn thing, one biochemist, and one spare historian who's just along for the ride. Maybe it's the breeze. Last night was still and overcast, whereas tonight is considerably less gloomy and breezier. That must make a significant difference to the background noise. Ears adjust their sensitivity in much the same way that eyes do, and they can play peculiar tricks on the town-bred. Your brain gets used to screening out familiar noises, but unfamiliar ones can seem very eerie when they become newly obtrusive. That was what spooked Jenny when we moved into the vicarage. I kept telling her that it was just a matter of adaptation, but she couldn't wait."

"Jesus, Doc, you really are full of bullshit sometimes," Pearlman told him. "I've spent a hell of a lot of time sitting in trees at night, and Claire's no novice. Did it ever occur to you that your wife had been living with you long enough for the seven-year itch to set in, and that she was suffering from an unease that had nothing whatsoever to do with the eerie silence of the countryside?"

Again, Hazard looked at Helen Hearne, who seemed to have spread the news of his personal circumstances around half the country. She was on her knees ostentatiously inspecting the heap of dirt that had murdered Moley.

"Let me take a look around," said Hazard. "If the beetles arrive—or moths, or anything else out of the ordinary, I'll be ready."

"They should be here by now," Pearlman muttered, obviously worried that the night-spirits were going to cheat him and stay hidden now that the skeptic had come to reckon with them. While he started rummaging in the dump, looking for a spare pare of rubber boots for Margaret Dunstable, Hazard slipped away into the darkness.

The crowns of the trees quivered in the breeze, as if in the grip of a sudden chill. With the aid of his flashlight Hazard had no difficulty locating the narrow passage through to the circle of flat ground surrounding Moley's "test-drill" and the rampart of excavated matter he'd built half way around it. Hazard took out his clasp-knife and extended the blade. No one had followed him along the improvised trail.

Gingerly, Hazard made his way across the open space to the edge of the hole. There were moths in the air, but no more than he would have expected to see on any summer night in any other woodland clearing. Bats were fluttering back and forth, but he couldn't see or hear any owls at present.

When he reached the rampart around the hole, Hazard played the beam of the torch over it methodically. There was some movement, but no beetle horde, nothing odd at all. After moving half way around the semicircle he stopped, and stood perfectly still, switched off his torch and tried not to make a sound, knowing that the darkness and the strain of keeping still would be bound to exaggerate the perceptions of his ears.

In such circumstances it would only be natural to sense communicative effort in the whispering of the branches, and he was on guard against it.

The darkness was profound; there were no fireflies here. The crowns of the trees continued to shiver and quake in the breeze. If the wood really did have a spirit, Hazard thought, it seemed to be coming down with something, perhaps vegetable meningitis.

Thirty heartbeats passed while Hazard savored the quality of the feverish whisper. It wasn't quite as clamorous as he might have expected—the density of the branches stifled the slight wind more effectively than he had anticipated. There were no birds moving in the crowns of the sickly trees, and it seemed that even the rats and mice preferred the regional hedgerows, because he could clearly hear a faint cacophony of scratching sounds, which he knew from experience to be the sound of hedgehogs moving through undergrowth and carabid beetles scurrying across the dried-out surface of leaf-litter. There might have been thousands of *Tenebrio* beetles following their own courses—or even taking line-dancing lessons—without their being able to add much to that slight symphony, because the discrepancy in size between the two kinds of insect was so very considerable, but there was still no indication of any unusual presence on the rampart.

After a while, Hazard continued around the rampart until he reached its terminus, and stood on the rim of the remaining semicircular edge of the excavation.

He shone the beam of his torch into the hole. It wasn't very deep; there didn't seem to be any danger of his being buried and asphyxiated if he lowered himself into it, but he didn't want to do that because it would have made his clothes horribly filthy, and although they were old ones, he didn't want to import black glutinous mire into his car while he drove home.

He used the clasp-knife to peck away at the rim of the hole, slicing off fragments and letting them fall to the bottom. Thanks to the patchy cloud cover the night wasn't cold especially within the canopy-blanketed wood. Hazard felt quite comfortable, although he put his hands flat upon his tracksuit top momentarily to take a hint of chill out of the fingers. There wasn't the remotest suggestion of any kind of uncanny presence, supernatural or biological, unless he was prepared to count the inflammation of the metaphorical sore spot that Steve Pearlman's last gibe about Jenny's desertion had touched.

It *had* occurred to Hazard that the business about not being able to stand the quietness and isolation of the Old Vicarage had been an excuse, and that what had really sent Jenny scurrying back to London was the awareness—brought out by closer confinement and the suspension of customary support systems—that she simply didn't want to spend the rest of her life with John Hazard, and might have found someone who seemed to be a more comfortable fit. That possibility still rankled, and it didn't need one of Pearlman's random darts to suggest that there might be more symbolic weight than ecological fascination in Hazard's fondness for the cemetery that lay between his home and the corpse of the church.

When Hazard switched his torch back on, the rampart was still innocent of any unusual presence, but as he swept the beam around he caught sight of a saucer-shaped depression in the flat surface, some ten feet away from the rim of the test-dig, where there did appear to be movement. He couldn't remember seeing it before, but that might simply be because it didn't show up as clearly in broad daylight. Perhaps it was the remnant of a belated puddle that had reappeared after the pond had been filled in because of seepage from below.

Intrigued, Hazard moved over the surface of the mire, apparently virgin of footprints, to the edge of the depression. There were indeed beetles in the saucer-shaped dent, including *Tenebrionidae*, but they were not present in anything remotely like the abundance that would have been required to allow Pearlman to fill the jar he'd loaded into Claire Croly's car as entomologist bait. Even so, they were there, and they were out of place.

Hazard suspected that Claire Croly would be able to quote numerous examples of instances in the rich history of psychic research when the presence of a single skeptic had been enough to banish all manner of paranormal phenomena that had been running riot while there were only true believers to bear witness, or at last reduce them to proportions that were only very slightly out of the ordinary. Perhaps that was what was happening here: the profusion that had been enormous the previous evening had been reduced to much more modest proportions in his level-headed presence: odd, but far from supernatural.

Hazard knelt down to inspect the saucer-shaped depression. He shifted the torch into his left hand and condescended to palpate the ground around with his right, even though he knew from glutinous experience what it might do to his fingertips. This time, however, the surface didn't seem sticky. Indeed, it felt strangely soft, as if he were touching skin rather than soil. After a moment's pause he laid his palm flat upon the ground, wondering why it didn't feel cold even though it was damp. Then he reached out into the depression in order to grab a handful of the beetles that were swarming there in hundreds.

The beetle host gave way under the pressure of his hand; perhaps he had dug into the mass more forcefully than he had intended, or harder than he had consciously intended. He gasped in surprise, although he tried to strangle the sound. The hand sank into the mass, which no longer felt like beetles running over a concave surface, or thick vegetable broth, or compacted earth, or anything that might have seemed remotely likely.

His hand vanished into the black surface, and he honestly had no idea whether it was being sucked into the mire or whether he was actually shoving it in with all his might. The only thing of which he was certain was that his body was twisting awkwardly as the arm descended, as he tried to find a stance that would enable him to remain balanced in his wellington boots rather than falling over on to his side or—far worse—forward on to his face. He was by no means sure how he managed that, without even shifting his feet unduly, because the arm disappeared all the way to the elbow and then beyond.

For one horrible moment, Hazard thought that the process, whether it was a pull or a push, might not stop, and that he might descend into the earth entirely, shoulder first, them torso and head, and finally—long after he had drowned or asphyxiated—pelvis and legs.

But no; the arm didn't descend entirely into the ground; the absorption came to a halt half way up the bicep.

The mud around his captive arm didn't feel cold. In fact, it didn't feel like anything at all; he had no sensation of his own arm as something separate and merely surrounded by something else, whether solid or liquid, inert or alive.

Awkward as it was, Hazard held his position while seconds dragged by—and then, perhaps, minutes. He lost track of time, although he didn't lose consciousness or even suffer from vertigo. He merely had a peculiar sensation of emptiness in his head, as if the environment of his thoughts had been strangely depleted, leaving his present train of thought and sensation oddly naked and isolated.

Eventually, the arm began to emerge again. This time he was fairly sure—almost certain, in fact—that he was actually pulling it out, although he was unaware of making any conscious effort to do so. He was exerting the force with his legs and his torso, not with the arm itself. He couldn't feel the arm itself at all; it was completely numb. He had the odd sensation that he sometimes experienced after going to sleep on his arm, that some kind of dead weight was dangling from his shoulder, without his being able to obtain any clear perception of its shape, position or nature.

Maneuvering the torch in his left hand, he played the beam over the entire length of the arm. The sleeve of the track-suit top was absolutely black, and seemed to be sopping wet. When he touched the sleeve, the fabric seemed bloated, and there seemed to be something squishy under-neath, which was not his arm but something surrounding his arm.

Hazard set the flashlight down carefully and used the thumb and index finger of the left hand to pull up the sleeve of the tracksuit-top by a few inches.

The arm underneath was as black as the fabric, but even as he watched, its shape seemed to shift, becoming more recognizably the familiar shape of his arm, no thicker than its usual plumpness. He dis-missed the idea that he had just seen some kind of slime being absorbed into his flesh as an optical illusion.

The arm was still completely numb, and the numbness did not seem to be wearing off, as it would have in an arm numbed by pressure from which the pressure had been removed.

It occurred to Hazard then that if the easing didn't start soon, he was going to have difficulty getting home. He couldn't drive with a dead right arm—not easily, at any rate.

"Shit!" he murmured, wanting to hear the reassuring sound of his own voice. "All things considered, a plague of beetles would have been preferable. This is just too weird for words."

He tried to analyze how he felt, but he couldn't. He didn't feel quite himself. He had the impression that his point of contact with the world—with the material universe and its baryonic contents—had subtly changed its nature, and that he had imported some perverse shadow of new meaning into the fundamental sensation of his existence. He knew that something was amiss, and that it was not the kind of thing he had tried to put himself on guard against when he had set out to investigate the mystery of the clearing.

"Dr. Hazard?" The voice, coming from the opening in the thicket at the edge of the clearing, was Claire Croly's.

The first thought that sprang into his mind—a naked, isolated thought, lacking the normal mental clothing provided by the virtual fabric of his mind—was that he did not want to become a case study in *Fortean Times*: a freak of nature, a damned datum, a cryptozoological phenomenon.

"Yes?" he answered.

"Are you all right?"

"Of course."

"Have you found something?"

"A few beetles. Ordinary beetles, in ordinary quantities. They do seem to have flocked to this saucer-shaped depression, but the cause of the gathering is impossible to determine."

"Pheromones?"

"I really don't know. We'll have to wait for the results of Helen's chemical analyses. But as I say, the numbers aren't extraordinary. Whatever you saw last night hasn't been repeated tonight—not here, at any rate. If Steve had found something elsewhere, he'd have shouted, wouldn't he?"

"I suppose so." The Fortean seemed chagrined, deeply disappointed by the poor quality of the phenomenon, as the entomologist had reported it.

Hazard rose to his feet, slowly, afraid that if he did so too rapidly he might suffer from vertigo. He directed the beam of the torch at patch of ground that had just swallowed his arm—he decided to think of it in those terms, even though he doubted their accuracy—but there was no visible trace of what had happened on the surface of the soil….if "soil" was the right word for something so strange. But "mire" was no better, and the "mini-peat-bog" he'd improvised while talking to Dennis Nordley was just silly. The beetles were still running around, though, with no good reason for being there, even in moderate quantities, and in spite of their known fondness for leaf litter.

He shone the beam on his arm again. The sleeve was still filthy, but it no longer seemed to be sopping wet. While not exactly dry—rather slimy, in fact—it no longer seemed as wet or as bulky as it had been.

"Have you hurt yourself?" Clair Croly asked.

"Not seriously," Hazard assured her. "I lost my balance and stuck my arm out to stop myself falling. I've jarred it a bit and got it absolutely filthy, but it'll be all right in a few minutes." He knew as he said it that it was a rather unscholarly fantasy, but it was a plausible story, worth sticking to and impossible to contradict.

"There are some paper towels at the dump," the reporter told him. "You can wipe off the worst of the muck there." She still hadn't moved from the narrow gap in the densely-patched circular wall of tangled saplings, creepers, brambles and parasites. By night, at least, perhaps without being conscious of the fact, she was unwilling to step on to the surface of the clearing.

Hazard hadn't had any such reluctance, but he had had a reason, an objective, in so doing. And anyway, as Steve Pearlman had said, the spirit of the wood liked him….

He cut off that lonely thought instantly. That way lay, if not madness, at least Fortean thinking: wild, undisciplined fantasy devoid of any but the most tokenistic scholarly dress. He tried, instead, to make a rational assessment of how he felt.

The arm was still completely numb; he couldn't feel it at all from half way down the upper section. He could still swing it from the shoulder, pendulum-fashion, so it wasn't paralyzed in the sense that it was stuck and immovable, but it was a dead weight, the hand and fingers devoid of sensation and the ability to obey any command from the brain to grip or carry out an action.

But how am I, in myself? Hazard wondered.

He wasn't sure. He wasn't even sure that he was wondering correctly, because although he was fully conscious and thinking rationally—seemingly, at least—there was still something odd about the environment of his train of thought, as if something in the background were missing—something that he could no more put his finger on metaphorically than he could have done so literally, just at present.

But I'm fine, he assured himself, sternly. *Fundamentally, I'm fine. I'm thinking clearly. I just have a dead arm, as if I'd jogged my funny bone. It will wear off. It will definitely wear off.*

Nevertheless, Hazard could not deny that felt a curious sensation within his own being, somewhere other than the precise location of his thought. It did not flow from the ground; rather, it seemed to begin deep in his own abdomen before reaching out into his limbs and through his extremities—not just the stunned arm and the temporarily-useless hand, but throughout his body, from his prickling scalp to his rubber-booted feet.

It's in my blood, Hazard thought, suddenly. *It's traveling throughout my body, but it's only paralyzed my arm, thank God. Now this really is interesting; this really is a phenomenon worth observing, worth analyzing, worth philosophizing about. But I'm the only one who can do it. I'm the only one who ought to do it. It's in me. It flowed right through my skin, by some kind of weird osmosis, the way that dimethyl sulfoxide acts as a carrier to transmit other molecules through the skin and into the blood. There's nothing supernatural about it—it's a known, studied, recognized phenomenon, with therapeutic applications. It hasn't been recognized in nature before, but that's all the more reason....*

"Are you sure you're all right, Dr. Hazard?" Claire Croly called.

"Absolutely," Hazard lied. "I just stumbled, and jarred my arm. It'll be okay in a moment. I need those paper towels, though, to clean up my sleeve as best I can. I'm coming back now."

He was walking even as he spoke. The reporter preceded him along the narrow trail. Branches brushed his face as he went, perhaps because he was slightly unsteady on his feet and couldn't keep himself as rigidly vertical as usual, or perhaps because the spirit of the forest liked him....

Again he shut down that temptation to silliness, and made his way back to the Last Ditchers' base, where Steve Pearlman was waiting, chatting to Margaret Dunstable. Helen Hearne was carefully placing stoppered glass tubes in the velvet-lined compartments of a carried designed to keep them safe from shock and breakage.

Good luck with that, Hazard thought, even though he was quite sure that he wasn't seriously broken, or even more than a tiny bit in shock.

Claire Croly found him a roll of paper towels, and he handed her his flashlight while he began methodically using his left hand to remove the residue of the black slime from the outer surface of his track-suit top.

"What happened?" asked Margaret Dunstable.

"I tripped and fell into the mire," Hazard told her, repeating his plausible story. "I put out my arm to stop myself, and hit a soft spot. It went in all the way to the bicep, but still took quite a jolt. The arm's numb, but nothing's broken. It'll be fine in a minute."

"He said that ten minutes ago," Claire Croly observed.

"I'm fine," Hazard assured them, as Steve Pearlman and Margaret Dunstable moved closer, showing concern. "It's just a case of the old fable about the astronomer walking along in the dark looking at the stars and falling into a hole, except that I'm a biologist looking for beetles and moths, and I just tripped and jolted my hand. Nothing's broken or even sprained."

"Are you sure about that?" asked the historian. "Maybe you ought to get it checked out at a hospital."

"Drive all the way to Newbury to visit A&E on a Saturday night, for a four hour wait among all the drunks? No thanks. It'll be fine. I'd know if there were anything seriously amiss. I might know more about insect anatomy than human anatomy, but I'd know if I'd broken anything, and even if it were a sprain, there'd be no point taking it to hospital."

Steve Pearlman, at least, still had his priorities in order. "Did you find anything, Doc?" he asked. There was no optimism in his voice.

"I found some beetles, and you only have to wave the torch around so see that there are moths flying—but not in unusual numbers."

"They were unusual last night," the ecowarrior insisted, doggedly. "You saw that jar. I didn't fake it. I didn't spend a week collecting the bugs just to trick you into coming on a fool's errand. There really is something weird about this place, and it has something to do with beetles."

"There's certainly something odd about it," Hazard agreed, "but even if there had been ten times as many *Tenebrio* in the clearing as there were, or a hundred times, we wouldn't be any further forward in figuring out exactly what. The samples Helen has collected might tell us more, once she's had a chance to put them through the mass spectrometer."

"You do realize that I'm only a postgrad," the biochemist put in. "I have to get permission and wait my turn. Dr. Nordley presumably doesn't have that kind of hassle, so he probably already knows what it'll take me days to figure out."

"But he has an interest in not seeing anything interesting, even if it's right in front of him," Pearlman asserted, "whereas we...."

"You're grasping at straws, Steve," Hazard old him. "Whatever we might find, or whatever you hoped we'd find, back in the beginning when you first roped us in, it's not going to cut any ice with DEFRA. They're going to spray the wood, and even if they weren't, there was never any more chance of having it declared a Site of Special Scientific Interest than an Area of Outstanding Natural Beauty. That cart track is going to be made into a neatly macadamed road with a white line down the middle and pavements to either side whether you like it or not, and in the fullness of time, your logic being all too plausible, it will be extended northwards on the other side of the hamlet that used to be a farm, and more houses will be built along the road on this side and that side, and the gradual erosion of the Green Belt will continue, inch by inch and mile by mile, and the air pollution will get worse and the climate will get hotter, and we'll all die a little bit sooner than we might have if we'd been living in New Jerusalem. There's no way to stop it; we just have to live with it as best we can."

Stubborn as he was, even Pearlman got tired. It was the middle of the night, and the clouds were obscuring the half-moon. The flashlight batteries were all getting tired as well. Everything was fading away, in its own fashion. The ecowarrior had not yet accepted the inevitable, but he was ready for a brief cease-fire in the eternal battle.

"I need to go home," Hazard added. "Helen, can you drive a Mondeo?"

"Of course," the biochemist said. "But am I insured to drive yours?"

"It's fine," Hazard assured her. "I got the extended cover so that Jenny could drive it."

"If your arm's so bad that you can't drive," said Margaret Dunstable, "I really think you ought to get it checked out at hospital."

"No way," said Hazard. "I need a shower and sleep, not a four-hour wait in Pandemonium. It's simple enough. Helen can drop me at my place, then take you home and take the car to her place. In the morning, she can drive it into campus and leave it in my usual parking spot. I'll be fine, and I won't need the car urgently, so I'll get a taxi in on Monday and pick up the keys from her in Biochemistry during the morning, so that I can drive to Sherfield to give my statement for the coroner. Everything will be sorted, back in its proper place....except for Steve, whose vocation is to be in the wrong place, at least until the police come to arrest him, on whatever charge they can trump up. Can we go now?"

"You're going to stay, right?" Pearlman said to Claire Croly. Again, there was no optimism in his voice.

"I think I've got all I need to write my article," the reporter told him. "More would have been nice, but I have enough. I need a shower and sleep too—it's been an eventful couple of days. I'll keep in touch."

Pearlman shook his head. It went without saying that he would stay. He would be on his own until his fellow ecowarriors came back with provisions, but that didn't frighten him. Perhaps it should have, even though, in Hazard's opinion, he wasn't in any real danger from imaginary night-spirits, but it didn't.

VII

The four of them walked back along the future road toward the A303. Margaret Dunstable didn't bother suggesting yet again that Hazard ought to go to A&E to be checked out. She knew the answer. It was Claire Croly who asked him: "Why do you think the beetles didn't show up tonight the way they did last night and the night before?"

"Perhaps they got what they wanted," Hazard said. "If it was some kind of pheromone mimic that brought them, it would only be a one-time thing. It wouldn't keep bringing them back repeatedly. Beetle sex-drives don't work that way. It might not happen again until next year—by which time...."

"It might never happen again," the reporter finished for him. "It's the bloody X-Files syndrome."

"What's that?" asked Helen Hearne.

"The curse of paranormal research. Every week, while the TV show was running, Mulder and Scully had to be confronted by some bizarre phenomenon, for which the bizarre explanation always turned out to be true, but the evidence for which had to disappear completely, so as not to change the backcloth to the series, that being the world we supposedly live in. It was the same with the old Night Stalker series: every week a new monster, every week all the evidence has to disappear at the end of the episode, so as to leave the world fundamentally undisturbed. It's the great curse of paranormal research. Things happen, but when the witnesses are summoned to see it, the events aren't repeated, so everyone goes home believing that they never happened the first time around—that it was just a hallucination or a hoax. Even when there is residual evidence, like that jar of insects in the boot of my car, it doesn't prove anything definite."

"The reason that TV series work that way has to do with the demands of fiction," Margaret Dunstable pointed out. "It's always been the same. Tall stories can't change the world, so they have to end by tidying away their innovations. In the real world, though, there's no such requirement. The phenomena ought to be repeatable and consistent, if they're real."

"Not according to what Dr. Hazard just said," the Fortean insisted. "Some things are essentially irregular—and not just the sex lives of beetles. Isn't there some kind of marine worm that only spawns one day a year, on a day fixed by the phases of the moon?"

"The Palolo worm," Hazard put in, helpfully.

"And it's not necessarily every year," the reporter persisted. "There are days when lots of cicadas hatch out all at once, not every year but at longer, irregular intervals—it's the same with locusts. And there are plants that only flower once every hundred years or threreabouts, and no one can tell when in advance. Right, Dr. Hazard."

"The plant example is outside my field," Hazard said scrupulously, "but in population dynamics, the examples of the Palolo worm and locust plagues are the tip of a very big iceberg. There are a great many phenomena that seem to follow approximate cycles, but which aren't precisely predictable. Even in my lab populations, it isn't possible to determine the duration of the various phases of the beetles' life-cycle with absolute precision, because eggs and pupae can both remain dormant for extended periods of time in response to what seem to be small variations in environmental circumstances. Things in nature aren't always as regular as they seem. There are certainly phenomena that only manifest themselves briefly, and then only repeat at intervals that we don't yet have the practical means to predict. It's the same with natural phenomena like volcanic eruptions; in some instances they seem to be approximately cyclic, but sometimes we can't find a pattern at all—although that doesn't mean that they're not entirely natural results of complex combinations of causes."

"So you see," said Claire Croly, "the fact the reported phenomena aren't repeatable on demand doesn't necessarily mean that the original reports were lies or mistakes. The fact that some people insist on dismissing all damned data, refusing to believe any of it, is as much a matter of psychology as the fact that some people cling to some beliefs of that sort with the conviction of faith. It's all very well to dismiss things as hallucinations or scholarly fantasies, with a shrug of the shoulders, so you don't have to think about them any more, but it's a good bet that some of those things that were and are dismissed were and remain true."

"The psychology of scholarly fantasies is an interesting area," Margaret Dunstable conceded. "Unfortunately, all the hypotheses that one can come up with to account for their nature, form and recurrence tend to be scholarly fantasies themselves…there's no way out of the maze. Not in history, at any rate, the past being dead and gone."

"But in biology," Helen Hearne observed, getting in ahead of Hazard, "there's always the possibility of new data turning up that will provide the evidential basis for converting the hypothesis into sound theory. It happens all the time—that's how we know that so many of the scientific ideas of the past were just pure fantasies, whereas some of the ones initially stigmatized as fantasies turned out to be correct. That's progress. Even in archeology, new evidence turns up continually that must destroy some historical fantasies and help to shore up others."

"That's true," Margaret Dunstable admitted. "Except that new evidence always tends to be interpreted in the light of existing theories, and when the theories are fantasies, they fantasize the evidence, slotting it in where it doesn't really belong and evading its destructive effects."

They had reached the lay-by, and it was time to go their separate ways. "I can give you a lift, Dr. Dunstable, if the logistics of using Dr. Hazard's car are too awkward," Claire Croly offered.

"No, that's all right," said the historian. "I'll go with John and Helen." She didn't say why, but Hazard suspected that it was because she was still concerned about his arm, which was still numb and useless, to the extent that he was beginning to doubt his own conviction that the condition was temporary.

As for the rest of him, he felt a little less strange. His mind, at least, seemed to be functioning perfectly normally, assisted by his discourse on discontinuities in nature. His thoughts no longer seemed to be operating in that curious mental isolation; they were in contact once again with his memories, and the other vague furniture of his consciousness. He didn't feel ill; in fact, he felt quite zestful, as if his metabolism had stepped up a gear.

The reporter from the *Fortean Times* bid them all farewell, without any undue effusion, and climbed into her Citroen. With his left hand, Hazard handed his keys to Helen Hearne.

"I'll get in the back," he said. "Unless you need me to navigate for you?"

"It's okay," the biochemist said. "I'm a scientist. I have a good sense of direction and a decent memory. I can get you both home without any difficulty. Your arm's no better, then?"

"It's wearing off now," Hazard said, with more optimism than accuracy, "but it's better to be safe than sorry. I think I could drive safely enough, but I shouldn't take the risk." He only had slight difficult getting into the car one-handed, although he had to be very careful to keep the black arm away from the seat, safely stowed in his lap. He didn't want to ruin the upholstery.

The vehicle pulled away, and headed back toward the old vicarage.

"You've had a wasted journey, I'm afraid," said Helen Hearne apparently addressing both of her companions. "I've got my samples, of course, but I really don't know whether I'll be able to find anything in them of any significance, and anything I do find will be of purely academic interest. Steve is going to have to count this one as a loss."

"He hasn't actually won any of them yet," Hazard pointed out. "It's been one fiasco after another. All he's ever contrived is to make a slight nuisance of himself—a mere gnat against the mighty juggernaut of development."

"He's quite an interesting fellow, though, in his way," said Margaret Dunstable. "I had a pleasant chat with him, so I don't consider the journey wasted at all. Your fall must have spoiled it for you, though, John?"

"Perhaps," said Hazard, a trifle hesitantly. In fact, he felt that the observation he had made, and was still making, was considerably more interesting than a temporary beetle invasion. Whatever was going on in Tenebrion Wood was utterly strange, even though he couldn't yet formulate a coherent hypothesis as to what it might be. Given that Denis Nordley was, as Steve Pearlman had pointed out, effectively being paid not to find anything interesting, he probably wouldn't, and poor Moley's encounter with the peculiar properties of the soil had proved fatal, but he had only dipped a finger in, metaphorically speaking, and he was actually taking away a part of the phenomenon for examination at length. That might end up making him a victim of the X-Files syndrome, with nothing to show for any hypothesis he did come up with but the memory of evidence that had disappeared, but at least he could investigate secretly, without putting his investigation or his job on the line. The important thing, after all, was to observe, scrupulously, before doing anything reckless.

His arm was still dead, though, and the persistence of that deadness was beginning to worry him. If whatever had flowed through his skin in liquid form had entered his bloodstream and been distributed throughout his body, there was no obvious reason why his arm was still leaden, unreactive to instructions sent from his brain and unable to transmit sensations thereto. Whatever was going on inside him was complex. It didn't seem to be doing the rest of his body any harm, and his mind seemed perfectly clear, lucid and sane, but his right hand was still offending him, because it was still to all intents and purposes cut off.

He wondered whether, if he weighed himself when he got home, he would find that he had put on weight, and, if so, how much. The problem was that was that he wasn't entirely sure how much he had weighed that morning. There was a set of scales in the bathroom, but he tended to think of them as "Jenny's scales" and hardly ever stood on them. He couldn't remember standing on them since Jenny had left, so he really didn't know how much he weighed. Since turning twenty-one he had thought of his "normal" adult weight as being somewhere in the region of twelve and a half stone—he'd never grown used to calculating in kilos—but the simple fact was that he had no sound baseline measurement for comparison. If he stood on the scales when he got home and the needle indicated thirteen stone, or even fourteen, he would have no real idea of the significance of the datum.

In any case, even if he could be certain that he was heavier now than he had been this morning, what would that signify, even to him, let alone to anyone else? He had put on weight. Big deal. People put on weight all the time, and often tried to blame it on exotic factors rather than admit that they simply ate too much and didn't do enough exercise. Any man who announced that he'd gained a stone or half a stone because some kind of strange liquid had flowed through his skin, with or without the aid of a transporter solvent like dimethyl sulfoxide, and had taken up residence within him like some kind of parasite, would simply make people think that he was deluded. Even readers of *Fortean Times* would laugh at him, and suggest he join a gym or enrol in Weight Watchers.

In any case, what real evidence did he have that that was actually what had happened to him? Was he really competent to judge that his mind was clear, lucid and sane? Was he really capable of drawing any reliable conclusion from what he thought had happened, given that he wasn't entirely clear as to what he did think? Had his arm been sucked into the mire, or had he pushed it in? He really didn't know. How reliable were the sensations he had had suggesting that something was entering into him? Completely unreliable. And even if something had somehow got inside him, penetrating the membrane of his skin like DMSO, what justified conceiving of it as something alive, some kind of parasite? Absolutely nothing. So far as he knew for sure, all that had happened was that his arm had got muddy, and then had gone dead, as if the blood circulation had been cut off, leaving the nerves unable to react. Except that the blood circulation hadn't been cut off—at least, he hoped not, because if it had, necrosis would be setting into the tissues of his hand by now.

He picked up his right hand in his left, and lifted it to the level of his face. It was dark inside the car, but the lights alongside the road were bright enough to reassure him that the hand, although still filthy, didn't seem to be rotting on the bones. Indeed, when he tried his utmost, he thought he could flex his fingers slightly. He took that to imply that some measure of sensation was returning, slowly.

I'll be fine, he told himself. *By morning, everything will be back to normal.*

He had closed his eyes in order to concentrate on trying to move his fingers, and he left them closed, trying to examine his state of mind more attentively.

Had the earth, or the wood, or the resident spirits of the wood, responded to his attempted investigation of it mystery? Had he attempted to look into the abyss only to find the abyss looking into him, as promised by the cliché?

Oh, shit, Hazard thought, realizing that he ought not to be thinking like that, that those were exactly the kinds of thought that he ought not to be entertaining. It was dangerous to think, even metaphorically, even jokingly, in terms of the spirit of the wood. The Old French *tenebrion* and the Old English *tenebrio* were futile concepts, mere figments of the imagination gone astray. He had to think in terms of biology, and if he were going to fantasize, he had to fantasize in biological terms.

He couldn't help feeling, though, that there might be times when intelligence was not enough, when rationality was not enough, and when even sheer bloody-mindedness might be unable to protect him from the waywardness of his own thought-processes, whether or not they were subject to external influence.

Carefully, he tried to think back to what had actually happened in the clearing. He tried to recall it to memory, so that he could assess it calmly and scrupulously.

He had reached down to look more closely at the *Tenebrio* beetles in the depression. He had reached out to touch them. He had lost his balance—or was that a retrospective deduction rather than and actual memory?—and he had put out his hand in order to prevent himself from falling on to his knees or his front and getting absolutely filthy....

At any rate, one way or another, his hand had plunged into the soft ground, which was so longer solid, having undergone some kind of a change of state...and the soil in the depression had been abruptly transformed, visibly and quite impossibly, into a seething mass of beetles: a plague of beetles that, for all he knew, might extend down to the very centre of the Earth. Instead of black soil that felt like the warm skin of some monstrous organism, there had been adult insects by the million: darkling beetles, every one. *Tenebrio* beetles, cursed by a coincidence of nomenclature to embody the spirit of Tenebrion Wood, at least in the impious mind and sinful eyes of a fallen entomologist....

No! None of that had happened. That was pure imagination—not even that, in fact. Somehow, while trying to think clearly and logically, his mind had drifted off into a sleep-state. Without ever quite losing consciousness, he had been subject to a swift nightmare, a brief irruption of the irrational into his ordered thought-processes. It happened. It wasn't even that unusual. It was late, he was drowsy, he'd had a trying day. He'd relaxed and closed his eyes, and his sense of purpose hadn't been adequate to keep the lapse into dream at bay.

But what if the nightmare was now tangled with his memories? What if, having suffered that brief invasion of sanity by disorder, his mental record of what had really happened was now confused, and permanently confused, so that he would never again be able to sort out, retrospectively, what was real from what was not? That sort of thing happened all the time, routinely. People did pick up false memories in exactly that fashion, almost invariably harmless ones, but not always....

"Are you asleep back there?"

The voice was Margaret Dunstable's.

"No," he said—although he knew full well that that was what people who had fallen asleep at inappropriate moments always said when challenged. Defensively, he added, also typically: "I was just thinking. I never lost consciousness."

That, at least, was true. He had never lost consciousness. The problem, if there was one, was the other way around. He had *gained* consciousness: false consciousness. But at least he knew that it was false. He knew what the truth was, behind the illusion.

Except that he didn't. He knew enough to reject the illusion—perhaps—but he really wasn't any closer to the truth, in spite of all his effort. He had no idea what had really happened to him...what was still happening to him.

The car door beside him opened. Margaret Dunstable was standing outside, holding it open from him.

"Well, we're here," she said. "Do you need a hand getting out?"

"No," said Hazard, a trifle brusquely.

He wormed his way out of the car.

"We really ought to have driven you to hospital," the historian said. "There are times when that masculine refusal to admit frailty needs to be overruled by sensible female *force majeure*. We should just have driven you to Newbury while you were asleep."

Hazard looked around. There was enough light to see the outline of the church, the wrought-iron gate to the cemetery, and his house. "Well, you didn't," he said. "I'm home now. I'll be fine.

He managed to fish his house keys out of his right trouser pocket with his left hand, and held them up triumphantly.

"See! No problem. "Helen can drop you off on her way home, and we'll follow the plan as mapped out."

"Absolutely not," said Margaret Dunstable. "I want to look at that arm when you've cleaned it up."

"You're not that kind of doctor, Dr. Dunstable," Hazard told her. "You're not competent to make diagnoses."

"Competent or not, if I think it looks bad, you're going to hospital, whether you like it or not. And it's Margaret now—old enough to be your mother, remember, and stepping in to fill the role because there's nobody else to do it. Now give those keys to me."

Hazard thought about refusing, but he could see the futility of starting a fight. It was better to get inside and negotiate from a stronger position. He handed over the keys.

Margaret Dunstable opened the door of the house, and all three of them went inside.

"Right," said the older woman, apparently assuming that having usurped power, she now had the prerogative of operating as an absolute dictator. "You put the kettle on, Helen. We'll go upstairs to the bathroom, John, where I'll make sure that you're able to undress and operate the shower by yourself, before I leave you to clean yourself up—but I'll be just outside the door, so you can call if you need help…or I can come in anyway if I hear anything untoward. No arguments. Once you're cleaned up, I'll take a good look at your arm."

Again, Hazard thought about refusing, feeling that the power-crazy woman was now exceeding her presumed authority in a fashion that was almost insulting—but the path of least resistance was simply to do what she said. He did need a shower, after all, and at least she wasn't insisting on watching him do it.

When the bathroom door was closed, after he had demonstrated that he was perfectly capable of taking off his clothes one-handed, he stepped on to the bathroom scales.

The scale read fourteen stone three pounds.

He was virtually certain that he hadn't been fourteen stone that morning, or anything like it, but he didn't have any proof of the fact.

He got into the bath, switched on the shower-attachment, and waited for the water to run hot. Then he moved into position and watched the residual dirt flow away from his numb arm as the jet fell directly upon it. The warm water seemed to restore some feeling to the flesh, but the limb was still dangling, and he could only twitch the fingers, without being able to grip anything.

Drying himself off wasn't as easy as undressing or letting the water of the shower run over him, but he managed it. There was a white toweling-fabric dressing gown hanging behind the bathroom door, which he put on. Then he opened the bathroom door and let Margaret Dunstable in. He allowed her to push up the right sleeve of the dressing gown. She picked up his inert hand and examined it carefully, palpating the fingers and the wrist, turning it back and forth. There was no bruising; the flesh looked quite healthy. She took his pulse, and although she didn't tell him the number to which she'd counted, she seemed satisfied. The mere fact that there was a pulse testified to the fact that the blood was circulating normally; there was no reason to fear necrosis.

"There's no obvious explanation for the paralysis," she observed, dubiously.

"It's not paralysis," Hazard told her. "The nerves have simply been stunned. There's no organic damage. The sensation, and the power of movement, will come back."

"How can you be sure?"

"Maybe I can't, but there's no reason to suppose otherwise. If it's still bad in the morning, there'll be time to think of taking it to the doctor then—but there's absolutely no reason to take it to A&E in the middle of the night."

She looked into his eyes, as if searching for further symptoms. He looked into hers, and saw, or imagined that he saw, long-frustrated maternal instincts, but he didn't make the observation aloud, because he thought he knew her well enough by now to know exactly how she would overreact, even though she wasn't quite as edgy as she had been earlier in the evening.

"Something happened," she said to him, as if she'd looked through his eyes into his mind. "Something more than you told us. Something *is* happening."

"Yes," he said. "I've got a dead arm for no obvious reason. Maybe there was something in the mud that had an anesthetic effect. It's as if I'd had a dose of lidocaine applied to my skin. It's unusual, but not inexplicable—and there's every reason to expect at it will wear off, exactly like any other local anesthetic."

"Very versatile mud, that," she observed. "Insect pheromones one night, lidocaine the next."

"If the water supply feeding the pond was corrupted by pesticide residues before drying out," Hazard said, fishing desperately for a better scholarly fantasy, "the residues left behind have probably continued re-acting and decaying ever since, and the bacteria seething in the decaying leaf litter have provided a bioreactor of sorts. Who can tell what Helen might find when she runs the stuff through the mass spec? My guess is that it's a real chemical jungle, and that the pheromone-mimic and the local anesthetic are just two out of many possible symptoms that might have turned up. It could have been a lot worse—imitation paraquat, or even something akin to sarin. But Steve's people aren't showing any skin rashes, and if poor Moley was poisoned before he drowned, the post-mortem will presumably turn up the evidence. As you can see, I'm thinking perfectly clearly. There's really no need to worry about me."

"All right," the historian conceded. "You don't have to tell me what you're hiding if you don't want to, obviously, and I don't have to give you a hackneyed lecture about problems shared being problems halved—but I am sincerely concerned, even though I'm not your mother and we only met less than forty-eight hours ago. One person is already dead, and I'm beginning to wonder whether that wood might really be dangerous."

"I'm fine," Hazard told her, stubbornly. For the moment, his predominant thought was that he wanted to be left alone, to think, and to recover: to straighten himself out, in more ways than one.

"Helen's made a cup of tea," the sincerely concerned woman told him. "When we've drunk it, we'll be on our way. You can come down as you are if you like, or put some clothes on. It's up to you."

"Thanks," said Hazard, again refraining from adding any sarcastic remark to which she might have snapped back with a hurtful verbal stab. While Margret Dunstable went back downstairs, he went into his bedroom in search of something slightly more respectable to wear.

The last thing he remembered, later, was bending down to open the second drawer down in the chest of drawers. He couldn't remember whether he had actually opened it or not, but he suspected the negative. At any rate, when he woke up, he was in bed, naked under the duvet.

VIII

Hazard had the sensation of having dreamed, and dreamed elaborately, for a long time, but he knew how deceptive such sensations were generally supposed to be by skeptical psychologists, and when he tried to remember exactly what he had been dreaming, the dreams fled and dissolved in his memory, leaving only fragments.

He remembered the sensation, if not the actual sight, of beetles swarming over his flesh in line-dancing legions, as if to seal a bargain by clasping it. They had started with his hand, swarmed up his arm, and then overwhelmed his whole body. For anyone else, that might have been a frightful nightmare, but Hazard was an entomologist. He wasn't afraid of insects, especially beetles, and he frequently dreamed about them. Indeed he sometimes suspected that he spent as much time counting beetles in his sleep as he did in his waking hours, just as methodically—except that he could never remember the numbers, and if he had written them down, it was only in imaginary notebooks.

He remembered, too, that Steve Pearlman had been in his dream. He thought he remembered him saying "I told you so!" but he wasn't at all sure to what the ex-student was referring, given that he had told him so many things over the years that they had been slightly acquainted. He thought Claire Croly had been in the dream too, but couldn't remember anything she might have said, and he was quite certain that it hadn't, at any point, been an erotic dream.

It had gone on and on, he thought, although not necessarily in chronological order. He remembered telling himself, probably repeatedly, that Adrian Stimpson's death really had been an accident—just one of those things, as the Dunstable had said; not murder and not human sacrifice, nothing to do with the vengeful spirit of the wood, which did not exist and never had. Nor, in spite of the fact that the mire and the damp ground surrounding it had been strangely warm, was there any rational basis for the idea he had formed in this dream that it might somehow be alive. That didn't make sense, and deserved to be discarded, and he had told himself that even in his dream, because he didn't stop being a scientist even in his sleep.

He remembered reminding himself, too, even in his dream, that as soon as the men in black from DEFRA had decided how much ground their spraying had to cover, every beetle in the wood would be living on borrowed time. To be harmless was no defense in that kind of war. To be as common as muck was no defense either. Come hell or high water, the path through the wood seemed to be destined to become a real road. The wood had avoided cultivation for more than a thousand years, but tarmac was too ultimate a weapon—and in law there was no such thing as a Site of Special Supernatural Interest.

Hazard dismissed all of that as the kind of stupidity to which dreams were always prone, even when a scientific conscience was struggling heroically within them. Five minutes of wakefulness, he thought, and it would all be gone forever, vanished into the swamp of forgetfulness.

He ran his hand over his forehead to smooth away some stray hairs—his right hand, he realized, belatedly.

He had been correct in his anticipation. The anesthetic effect had worn off. The local anesthetic had lost its effect. He was back to normal.

He opened his eyes, but the curtains hadn't been drawn over the bedroom window and the sunlight was streaming in. He closed them again while he eased his way out from under the duvet and headed for the door. He crossed the corridor into the bathroom, and begun his morning routine. Before getting into the shower though, he stepped on to the bathroom scales.

Twelve stone ten: not much different from what he thought of as his normal weight.

Had he made a mistake the previous evening, then? Had he been deluded when he had thought he saw the needle indicating more than fourteen stone? Had he been so possessed by the idea that his body had been invaded that he had actually misread the figure in line with his fears?

"Probably," he said to himself, aloud. He looked down, inspecting his body. Everything seemed normal, still definitely on the plump side of athletic, but not bad, all things considered—better, in fact, than he had expected. After all, he was an academic, not a long-distance runner or a body-builder.

He stepped into the bath, pulled the shower-screen across and turned the water on, standing to one side until it began to run hot. Then he stepped under it, and slowly turned around.

He almost failed to notice the blood running down the plug-hole, and only caught the merest glimpse of it before it had disappeared—and then, he was no longer sure that it had been blood. Had it not been another mistake, a belated flash of his turbulent dreams invading wakefulness for a split second?

He inspected his body again. He couldn't see his back, of course, but he felt it. There was no sign of any tenderness or injury, no part of it where his touch provoked a twinge of pain. Had it been an illusion, then?

"Must have been," was his judgment this time, again voiced aloud in order to make it seem more certain than he was really capable of being.

He reached, automatically, for the dressing-gown that should have been hanging on the back of the door.

It wasn't there.

He remembered the having put it on the night before, and then going into his bedroom, after which….

A blank.

Presumably—logically—the dressing-gown must still be in the bed-room, where he must have shrugged it off before collapsing into bed, so dog-tired that he couldn't remember doing it.

He remembered bending down over the chest of drawers…and then nothing.

No matter, he thought, there being no point this time in saying it aloud.

He walked out of the bathroom intending to go across the corridor into his bedroom, but stopped dead in the doorway and nearly jumped out of his skin.

Margaret Dunstable was standing in the corridor, between the bath-room and the bedroom. She was fully dressed—which observation re-minded him that he wasn't. He cupped his hands and covered what he could cover, fully aware that the reflexive action must look exceedingly comical.

"It's all right," said Margaret Dunstable. "In spite of my preferences, I've seen male genitalia before; they don't appall me any more than they excite me. I presume, though, that your right hand has fully recovered its normal abilities?"

Hazard didn't even attempt to answer her until he had dodged around her, gone into the bedroom, found the dressing-gown where it was lying on an armchair, and put it on. Then he turned round. She was standing on the threshold, the bedroom door being wide open.

"What the *hell* are you doing here?" he demanded.

"I slept in the spare room," she said. "I didn't think it was safe to leave you. I intended to check on you at regular intervals, but I have to admit that I slept more soundly than I expected."

"Helen was supposed to take you home. That was *agreed*."

"Yes, but that was before you collapsed. I wanted to call an ambulance, but Helen talked me out of it. Your pulse and breathing seemed fine, so we just picked you up and put you to bed."

"Stark naked?"

"No need to worry. Helen might not have my preferences but she didn't seem appalled or excited either. She did go home though, when I volunteered to stay and monitor your condition. I nearly called the ambulance as soon as she'd gone, but by that time you looked as if you were simply asleep, and you hadn't even bumped your head when you fell, so I wasn't entirely sure that I could explain to the ambulance crew why I'd called them out all this way on a Saturday night. On balance, I thought that it was better to let sleeping dogs lie, as it were, and monitor the situation at regular intervals…which, as I've just admitted, I didn't quite manage to do. But at least you're all right…except…has that bloodstain on the carpet by the bed been there for some time?"

Hazard looked down. There was indeed a small brownish patch on the rag beside the bed, which looked like an old bloodstain. He was reasonably certain, however, that it had not been there last time he had looked at the rug. He had no clear idea when that might have been, but he was sure that he would have noticed in passing…except, obviously, that he hadn't noticed it earlier that morning, when he got out of bed squinting against the bright light.

Hazard simply stood still, bewildered. Margaret Dunstable marched over to the bed and pulled away the duvet. Then she gasped. Obviously, she was looking for bloodstains, and that was what he had found—but she had not expected a lake. The sheet and mattress bore an elliptical stain more than a foot in the long diameter, and at least eleven inches in the shorter one. But she had seen Hazard's naked body, from the front and the back, and knew that he had no open wound. That was presumably why she looked at him in frank amazement and said: "Where did all that come from?"

"I have no idea," he said—but that was a lie. He did have an idea; he just wasn't prepared to voice it. He knew now that there really had been blood running down the plughole in the shower, and that he had washed it off his back. The bloodstain had come from him—it but it hadn't flowed from a cut. It had come through his skin, transported as a solute by something akin DMSO, to which skin was permeable—something exceedingly odd. He hesitated even to subvocalize the word *alien*. But knew that it was there, in the back of his mind. He didn't feel faint, though, and when he glanced at the wall mirror, he didn't seem unusually pale or thin. If he had lost a lot of blood, he wasn't feeling the expectable effects. Perhaps his bone-marrow had manufactured more during the night, or perhaps the stain was bulked out by other substances than blood.

Margaret Dunstable was probing the stain with her finger, cautiously, but Hazard knew that she didn't have any stocks of knowledge that would permit her to make any deductions from her investigation, except for the fact that he had bled. One way or another, that was all that there was to it: he had bled.

Except that it wasn't. He was pretty sure that he hadn't got out of bed all night, but there was also a bloodstain on the rug. And….

"It's dry," the historian said. "It looks quite old, although it can't be. It wasn't there last night, when we put you to bed." She too had deduced its origin, although the fact must seem even more mysterious to her than it did to him.

"It might not be blood," said Hazard, tentatively, although he knew that the possibility didn't lessen the mystery in the least.

Margaret Dunstable was already inspecting the bedroom floor. "I think there's a trail, of sorts," she said.

It wasn't obvious, but she was right. When Hazard knelt down and looked at the rug and the carpet beyond its edge, he could see that there were, indeed, faint traces in a dotted line that led toward the door…and beyond.

The door had been closed, of course, but there was a crack underneath it. Whatever had made the trail had gone under the door…or *flowed* under the door. Even though she was no biologist, Margaret Dunstable was capable of deducing that, and probably capable of taking the chain of conjecture further.

But so what? Hazard thought. *She's not an enemy. We're on first name terms. She's seen me naked. And she's an expert on scholarly fantasy.*

He now felt quite certain that the bathroom scales had not lied, at any point in recent history, and that he had not hallucinated any of their readings. There had been something inside him the previous evening, which was no longer inside him. It had flowed into him and flowed out of him, and it had flowed out of his bedroom and then, he assumed, down the stairs.

But it had not done him any harm. It had even used a local anesthetic to take possession of him. By demonic standards, that definitely qualified as polite. Night-spirits, or their biological equivalent, evidently had diplomatic protocols.

Now, it was gone, and the evidence it had left behind was so vague as to be utterly unpersuasive. It was Claire Croly's X-File syndrome all over again. Not that Hazard had any intention of ever trying to persuade someone of the truth of what had happened to him, or even letting on. It was a private matter, which, he couldn't help feeling, should have been for his eyes and his mind only.

Unfortunately, it wasn't.

Margaret Dunstable was following the blood trail—with some difficulty, because it was very faint indeed on the stair carpet, and by the time she got to the bottom, it seemed to have vanished completely. She looked along the corridor at the front door, then sideways at the sitting-room door and then round the corner at the kitchen door, but didn't seem to be able to pick up the trail again.

"I think we'd better have a cup of coffee," she said, looking up at Hazard, who was still standing at the top of the stairs, "and some breakfast. I'll do it while you get dressed. Then we need to have a serious discussion."

By the time that Hazard came downstairs—because he didn't hurry—Margaret Dunstable had already poured him a cup of coffee, made four slices of toast and put another two into the toaster. It was a trifle Spartan, but no more so than the Camembert and rye crackers that Hazard normally had for breakfast. He thought about getting the cheese out for the fridge but decided that it would seem impolite, and settled for spreading butter and marmalade on the toast, while the historian did the same.

Eventually, she said: "I knew you were hiding something last night, but I couldn't imagine what it was. Now I know why I couldn't imagine it, and I suppose I can understand why you didn't mention it. Were you actually aware of the fact that some kind of organism had stuck to you? I assume that it *had* stuck to you, even though Helen and I couldn't see it when we lifted you into bed last night. It was extremely well camouflaged.

"I wasn't exactly sure what had happened," Hazard said, slowly, "and I'm not much wiser now." He hesitated for a moment, but figured that she had already seen, and said, too much for him to exclude her completely. He had nothing to lose by telling the truth. "And I don't think it was *stuck to me*," he added. "I think it was actually inside me."

"And how did it get there?" she said, evidently trying not to seem too incredulous. "Did you swallow it?"

"No. It inserted itself through the skin of my arm."

"That's hard to believe."

"Yes, it is. I'm still finding it hard—but that was what happened, or seemed to."

"How is that possible?"

"Skin is permeable to some organic compounds, including dimethyl sulfoxide, which is also a powerful solvent, and can carry substances dissolved in it through the skin and into the bloodstream. It has various uses in medicine for introducing therapeutic compounds when there's a clinical reason for avoiding hypodermic injection."

"I can see that that might be a useful trick for a parasitic organism to have," the historian admitted.

"I'm not sure that what we're talking about here necessarily qualifies as an organism," Hazard told her. "Not, at any rate, an organism possessed of cells and membranes. In order to infiltrate in the fashion I've just suggested, the organism would probably have to be in a liquid state, colloidal at the very least. That's how it gets under doors too."

"Liquid life," said his historian, nodding her head as if the fantasy were easy enough to take aboard.

"Not necessarily liquid all the time. Perhaps capable of changes of state—an extreme kind of metamorphosis."

"We're talking about an alien life form, right?"

"That depends what you mean by *alien*—and, I suppose, exactly what you mean by *life*. Not like most of the life-forms we've so far classified, certainly, although there are some bacteria without cell walls that might qualify as fluid…but there's no need yet to start thinking in extraterrestrial terms. It's something unfamiliar, certainly, but I'm not prepared yet to consider it entirely external to our way of thinking. Such entities would be difficult to detect, of course—which may be why they haven't been detected…except by people who didn't talk about it, for the same reason that you and I aren't going to talk about it."

"We aren't?"

"Not immediately, at any rate. Not without hard evidence…and hard evidence for liquid life—if life is the right word—is, virtually by definition, something that's not easy to produce. Even if the elements of its chemistry showed up on the analyses that Dennis Nordley and Helen Hearne might be able to carry out, there wouldn't be any way to demonstrate that they're part of a complex system. And an entity that can effectively dissolve itself in mud is just going look like mud to most inquiring eyes. I can't imagine that invading human beings is part of its normal life cycle, but if it occasionally does that, as I say, people who talk about it probably aren't believed, and some might not even notice it, or recognize it as an invasion, any more than people in the past who fell ill as a result of bacteria or viruses recognized that as an invasion for most of human history."

"Would viruses qualify as liquid life?" the historian asked, still in quest of a way to get a conceptual grip on the entity. "Is this thing more like a virus than a cellular organism?"

"There are analogies that might be drawn," was all that Hazard felt ready to admit, as yet. "Viruses call the definition of life into question because they can't reproduce themselves without hijacking another organism's genetic system, and some of them undergo changes of state—the term *crystalline virus* was once quite common, or even *colloidal crystalline viruses*, although I've always been suspicious of scholarly fantasy in such cases...."

"But that's where we are at the moment," the historian pointed out. "You have to fantasize in order to come up with a testable hypothesis... and if you can't fantasize with sufficient ingenuity, you won't be able to do that."

"I know," he said. "And if you can't formulate a plausible hypothesis, or if you lack the means to do the crucial test, it remains a fantasy—an X-File, or a damned datum, in Claire Croly's jargon—forever." He chewed toast and marmalade reflectively, hoping that the sugar would kick in soon and give his brain a necessary boost. Then he took a liberal swig of coffee, figuring that the caffeine might help too.

"I see what you mean about people falling ill," said Margaret Dunstable, after imitating him, perhaps unconsciously. "Even now, people just experience it as falling ill, and rely on expert diagnosis to figure out whether it's a bacterium, a virus, or....we really don't know, do we, whether there are other alternatives, or what they might be? Perhaps some of the things we routinely attribute to viruses, because that explanation is available, are really due to something else...assuming, that is, we can't think of this thing as a kind of virus?"

Hazard shook his head, more in puzzlement than because he could rule the analogy out conclusively. A virus weighing several pounds, which flowed into a metazoan body and then flowed out again was—he almost laughed aloud at the internal thought—difficult to swallow, but, on the other hand, if there really were colloidal crystalline viruses, compounded from the aggregation of millions of virus particles, it wasn't inconceivable that there might be leviathans of the species, compounded out of billions....

He became aware that his companion was looking at him expectantly, wanting him to think aloud. He tried to organize his ideas into an appropriate condition for vocalization.

"Obviously," he said, "what happened to me last night was unusual, although it might not be unprecedented, past instances simply having dissolved into the general background of experienced disease, construed as temporary paralyses. Whatever exists in the pond in Tenebrion Wood is exceptional, but it might—perhaps must—have less obtrusive kin that have been living alongside us throughout history, unobserved because they've been unobservable prior to the modern era, and haven't yet crossed the threshold of observability that permitted us first to discern bacteria, and then viruses."

"You've just observed one, though," the historian pointed out.

"The problem is that one observation isn't enough. A scientific fact requires repeated, consistent observations. Even then...hundreds of sightings of yetis, sasquatches and unicorns—the entire cryptozoological encyclopedia—are only enough to reach the pages of *Fortean Times*. To get into the pages of *Nature*, you have to catch one—preferably alive, because dead ones can be faked."

"Like Jenny Hanivers," Margaret Dunstable supplied.

"Exactly," said Hazard, not needing her to explain to him that Jenny Hanivers were fake mermaids, once manufactured in some quantity to supply eighteenth century cabinets of curiosities. "And then, there's a whole other realm of Fortean fantasies...the delusory."

"That blood trail isn't a delusion," Margaret Dunstable assured him. "You can take my word for that."

"But what does it prove, taken in isolation, without my particular testimony to establish its oddity? And what is my particular testimony worth, even to you? How can even I be sure of the extent to what I experienced was real? I'm perfectly certain that it was polluted by dream-imagery to some extent, and there's no way to draw a clear line between the elements forced on my sensation from outside and those my own mind generated in trying to grapple with it as it happened. Maybe the entire impression of being invaded was just a product of my own mind—when I first realized that my weight had changed, in fact, my immediate reaction was to think that I'd made a mistake last night, and that I hadn't actually been fourteen stone at all. Perhaps that's still the most likely explanation, and none of this is real."

"Except the bloodstains," the historian related. She was, however, quick to add: "Which, as you say, aren't worth much as evidence in isolation. They don't prove anything...unless we can catch the thing that made them. If it's still in the house...."

"But we can't catch it, any more than we could catch a virus that had given us a cold in the head and then moved on. It's big, apparently, but even if we could tell which way it went, once it stopped leaking blood, what could we find when we caught up with it except a damp patch in the carpet? Just mud, that could have been tracked in on my feet, even though I put the wellingtons back in the boot."

"Not *just* mud."

"No, but remember what Helen said yesterday about it being one thing to know how genes code for proteins, and quite another to know how organisms use those elements to build a structure. Knowing the constituents of the mud doesn't tell us anything about how those constituents are organized in such a way as to constitute something more complex than the sum of their parts. It's not just a matter of finding the entity—it's a matter of seeing it in action...experiencing it in action...demonstrating that it can do to others what it did to me...whatever that was, exactly."

"But if we can find it....," Margaret Dunstable insisted.

"And if we can identify it if we do, and if we can collect it, assuming that it's anything more than a mere stain, and still capable to reproducing its action...and then, for light relief, we could try to catch the wind, or the sea in a sieve.

"The blood on your mattress can't be just ordinary blood, though—the kind you'd have shed if you'd cut yourself. Wouldn't analyzing the stain prove something?"

"It might tell us something—give us further clues as to what this entity is made of—but it wouldn't prove anything. A stain is still just a stain. Even if the hemoglobin has other organic compounds mixed with it, which don't normally occur in the human body, what would it prove? There's a big imaginative leap between showing someone a bloodstain that has other substances mixed with it and asking them to believe, in consequence, that it was caused by a liquid entity that oozed into my body from a miry pond, and oozed out again once it had drunk its fill of my nutrients. You formulated the hypothesis before I did, and I confirmed it for you—but can you put your hand on your skeptical heart and tell me that, after thinking about it rationally for a day or two, you'll really be able to believe it?"

Margaret Dunstable didn't actually put her hand on her heart, nor did she point out, pedantically, that it was actually her mind that was notoriously skeptical, but she did think about it for a few moments, while she demolished the last of the toast and drained her coffee cup. Eventually, she said: "I do believe you, in fact—but I'm old, and starved of intellectual stimulation, ready prey for scholarly fantasy in spite of my reputation. I'm not sure that anyone else would believe it, on the evidence you've shown me—except, obviously, Claire Croly."

"Claire Croly is a reporter for *Fortean Times*. She's paid to pretend to believe six impossible things before breakfast...or at least to take them seriously enough to report them. Not only wouldn't her credence help to convince anyone else, it would actually deter them from taking the hypothesis seriously. And just because we're batting around terms like *crystalline colloidal virus* doesn't mean that it really qualifies as a scientific hypothesis. What grounds do I have, in the final analysis, for using that kind of terminology rather than simply saying that there really are vampire goblins in the wood, and that one of them possessed me in order to feast, rather messily, on my blood? All I've done, really, is accommodate what I thought I experienced to my framework of under- standing…but even now, bloodstains and all, it's just a scholarly fantasy. It can't be any more."

"But if it's real—if it exists physically, if it really has a life-cycle, then it *must* be possible to demonstrate that it exists: to capture it, to investigate it."

"Of course," said Hazard, "but it isn't going to be easy."

"You are going to investigate, though?"

Hazard was mildly surprised that she even thought it necessary to ask, although the question was presumably rhetorical. "Of course. I'm a scientist—what else would I do? I guess I'm now a mad scientist, in the saddle of a crazy hobby-horse, and I'm going to be spending a lot of time with bucketfuls of black mire, trying to tease the life-forms out, and trying to figure out the whole range of tricks they can play, while the onlookers who thought I was a little bit mad even when I was count- ing flour-beetles think I've flipped and one completely cuckoo. It might take a lifetime, but I'm certainly going to give it a go. How could I do otherwise?"

"Knowing all the while," said the historian, reflectively, "that that's exactly what scholarly fantasists typically do. First find your chimera…."

She wasn't mocking though. There was an irony in that, Hazard knew. The expert on scholarly fantasy, who irritated everyone she knew by casting scrupulous doubt on their cherished convictions, might be the only person in the world, barring Claire Croly and her Fortean kin, who was able to sympathize with what he felt he had to do. She understood the psychology of his situation—and also understood that all hypotheses had to start out as fantasy, including the ones that ultimately stood up to experimental testing.

"I'll have to hurry gathering the raw material, though." he added. "Once DEFRA get around to spraying insecticide all over the place, the already-endangered species might become extinct before its existence is even recorded. Mercifully, it's Sunday—and administrative red tape being what it is, I'll probably have the best part of a week in hand. I'll certainly be back there this evening, though, for when the things come out at night."

"Are you going to tell Steve Pearlman?"

"I'm not sure that I dare. He'd be bound to blab, at least to Claire Croly, and make the whole thing public while I don't have anything to defend myself against becoming a laughing-stock. It does seem a trifle unfair not to tell him, but discretion might be the better part of valor in this instance. I'll tell him that I'm going back to investigate the beetles further. It won't be a lie. He'll be pleased—and if and when I have something provable, I'll make sure that he's one of the first to know."

Margaret Dunstable had continued thinking while he was talking. "You think the beetles must be part of the entity's usual life-cycle, I suppose? That it tricks them into gathering together so that it can infiltrate them, and thus get distributed, in much the same way that bees distribute the pollen of flowers?"

"It might fit the picture I'm trying to build," Hazard conceded, cautiously, "but I need to be careful to keep a wide-open mind. If that were the case, these things would be quite common—but who's to say that they aren't, given that they're so difficult to detect, or at least to distinguish? If they normally employ beetles and moths as carriers, most of them must be microscopic, but impossible actually to detect looking down a microscope, because they have no discernible cellular structure. Maybe what got in me last night is just a vast colony of tiny creatures, analogous to a slime-mold, or maybe it's the giant of the genus, the titan of liquid life. With luck, time will tell. In the meantime, I can't call it an undine, since I now know that elementals are a seventeenth century scholarly fantasy, but I can't call it a virus either, because that would be taking too much for granted, and even calling it a life-form or an organism might be saying too much."

"It's going to take me time to digest all this," the historian observed, "but I'm not such an old bitch that I can't learn a few new tricks. I can certainly understand your reluctance to go public before you've figured out a way to prove any assertions you make, and to play your cards close to your chest. I suppose I'm lucky that I stayed here last night and discovered the bloodstains—otherwise you'd have excluded me, too, wouldn't you?"

Hazard couldn't deny it, so he didn't. "Was it luck?" he said, instead. "Where, exactly, does the good fortune come into it?"

She stared at him, hard. "I'm content to call it luck," she told him, eventually. "At my age, you're grateful for any new ideas, even new scholarly fantasies. They keep monotony at bay. It's not exactly my field—but then, it's not exactly yours either. I'm not much of a lab assistant, but that doesn't mean that I can't help."

"You want to help?"

"Of course. Isn't that why you've told me all this, instead of fobbing me off with smoke and mirrors. Unless, of course, it *is* smoke and mirrors and you're really nursing an entirely different hypothesis."

Hazard had think about that for a few seconds, but decided that she was at least half right. He had talked to her about it because he wanted to talk about it, if only to get it straight in his own mind, and she happened to be there. He had been fishing for moral support, if not practical assistance. Obviously, he couldn't talk about it to Steve Pearlman, or to any of his colleagues in the department, and certainly not to the likes of Claire Croly; he didn't have Jenny any more, so who else could he look to for that support? There was Helen Hearne, but…well, he would have to make up his mind about that, but for the time being, it might be as well that she hadn't seen anything significant and, so far as he knew, didn't suspect anything. He would need the results of her analyses, though, and maybe a lot more, so perhaps a *folie à trois* would be even better than a *folie à deux*, provided that the expansion of the crazy secret could stop there….

It was at that moment that Hazard heard a car coming up the lane to the church. He wouldn't necessarily have been able to tell the sound of his own engine in a thousand, but he didn't have any difficulty jumping to the right conclusion.

IX

"That's Helen," Hazard said to Margaret Dunstable, not knowing whether he ought to feel alarmed or glad, but unable to prevent a hint of annoyance showing in his voice. "She wasn't supposed to bring the car back—that wasn't in the plan."

"She probably wants to find out how you are," Margaret Dunstable suggested, mildly. "She might not have been appalled or excited by hauling your naked body on to your bed once we'd taken the dressing-gown off—with difficulty, I might add—but she was probably sufficiently upset to be worried about you.

"Probably," Hazard admitted.

The doorbell rang.

"I'll get it," Margaret Dunstable volunteered.

A few moments later, the biochemist came into the kitchen, without the historian.

"Why is there a huge bloodstain on your doorstep?" she enquired.

Again, Hazard didn't know whether to be alarmed or glad. He hesitated, and then procrastinated. "Nobody's been murdered," he said. "I think the blood's mine."

"You *think*? If I'd bled like that, I'd know."

"Actually," he said, wryly, "I'm not at all sure that you would."

Margaret Dunstable reappeared them. She looked at Hazard, gave Helen Hearne a significant sideways glace, and then looked back, interrogatively.

Hazard shrugged his shoulders, and nodded his head.

"What I think happened," the historian said, "is that it only left faint traces on the stairs in the hall because it was on the move—it wasn't actually running out of blood to leak. When it got outside into the open, it paused—probably for quite some time, leaking or excreting while it waited. Then it set off again…I suppose it would be a step too far to say that it had decided which way I go?"

"I would think so," Hazard agreed. "It probably has some sensory capacity, though, and the ability to respond to chemical stimuli. Even amoebas can do that. Do you know which way it went?"

"Straight across the road and into the graveyard. Once through the gate, it's impossible to tell, all the more so because the grass is slightly damp with dew. We ought to look for it, though, just in case."

"I guess," Hazard agreed, although he didn't immediately leap to his feet. Sugar and caffeine notwithstanding, he didn't seem to have much get-up-and-go now the adrenalin produced by the initial shock had worn off. Perhaps that wasn't surprising if he had donated a pint of blood to the…entity.

"There are plenty of insects in the undergrowth, though," Margaret Dunstable added. "It might be interesting to go over there at dusk, before we head off to Tenebrion Wood."

"I get the feeling I'm missing something," said Helen Hearne, with more than a slight hint of annoyance in her tone. "*What* sat on the door-step leaking and then made a run for the graveyard?"

"The thing that hitched a ride in my arm out of Tenebrion Wood last night," said Hazard, briefly, throwing caution to the wind, while promising himself that it would be the last time. Three might prove to be a crowd, but it was probably a sustainable crowd, in the circumstances, and a biochemist would certainly be useful to him if he really was going to ride the hobby-horse all the way to the finish line.

"*In* your arm?" the biochemist queried.

"A liquid entity of some kind. It used the natural permeability of skin to certain organic solvents and their solutes to invade my arm."

The postgrad thought about it for a minute, but she clearly wasn't out of her intellectual depth yet. "And when it left again," she said, "it took a pint of your blood with it?"

"Apparently. The hemogolobin, at least."

"So Steve's wood is a Site of Special Scientific Interest after all? And you didn't tell him?"

"I hadn't worked out what had happened last night. I'm still not en-tirely sure—but I do know that it's not going to be easy to prove. And while I'm vulnerable to being treated as a complete lunatic, I don't want the story spread around. Can you live with that?"

"I'll make you a cup of coffee while you think about it, dear," said Margaret Dunstable, helpfully. "Would you like some toast?"

"No thanks," the younger woman replied. "I've had breakfast. So this is a committee meeting is it? And you're offering to let me in, pro-vided that I don't talk about it—to Steve or anyone else?"

"That's about the size of it," Hazard conceded. "Not that I'm in any position to lay down conditions—but I'd rather you were discreet, be-cause it could seriously mess things up for me if you aren't. You must know Professor Pilkington by reputation. It will be bad enough if he hears that I've been trespassing in Tenebrion Wood—how do you think he'll react if he thinks I'm telling people that I was invaded by some exotic biological entity while I was there? Even if it's true—especially if it's true."

Helen Hearne sat down, and Margaret Dunstable handed her a cup of coffee. She put two more slices of bread in the toaster anyway, presumably deciding that she needed more brain-fuel herself.

After a few moments, the biochemist said: "If you're serious, this is an opening to a whole new field of zoology. Claire Croly would probably give her proverbial eye-teeth for the story. It's what *Fortean Times* would reckon as a scoop. Not just liquid life but liquid vampire life. A double whammy."

"Fortunately," Hazard observed, dryly, "she doesn't have a *News of the World*-sized budget, so she can't pay you for the story."

"I wouldn't sell it to her if she could," the postgrad insisted, putting on a pretence of being offended. "I'm a scientist, not a whore. I can understand why you might want to keep it quiet, precisely because of the Fortean double hit. Instant backlash, followed by pariah status. Not to mention, as you say, that you'd be admitting trespass, with a pissed-off landowner in the wings waiting for an excuse to pounce. But you can't allow DEFRA to spray the wood while they're annihilating the Colorado beetle."

"Do you think I can stop them?"

"Is that why you're going back to the wood tonight—with bigger specimen jars? You don't think you can catch the one in the graveyard?"

"How? And if I could, what would it prove? You've got half a dozen specimen tubes full of mud, which could be crawling with liquid entities capable of burrowing into your skin—but if they are, how can you demonstrate the fact?"

The biochemist took a swig of coffee, and frowned. "The thing that left that blood on the doorstep must be big. Did you actually *feel* it going into your arm?"

"No," said Hazard. "It seems to have had the advantage of something akin to lidocaine, like the anesthetic mosquitoes inject when they bite. I didn't feel a thing for a long time. I suspect that the anesthetic didn't wear off until the invader had made its exit. A very discreet vampire, if that's really what it is…but the most efficient parasites are the ones that don't do their hosts any harm."

The postgrad nodded, having no difficulty following the logic. After a pause, she asked: "How much danger are we in, do you think?"

"Danger of what?"

"Infection, of course. Just because something sizeable has come out of you doesn't mean that it hasn't left its eggs behind. Meaning no offense, Dr. Hazard, but right now you could be the new Typhoid Mary."

Hazard hadn't thought of that, although he realized right away that he should have. Margaret Dunstable hadn't thought of it either but she had an excuse. She was accustomed to a very different range of scholarly flights of fancy, all essentially harmless. Now, plainly, they were both bearing in mind the fact that they had laid hands on his naked body the previous evening, presumably still a trifle damp from the shower, if nothing else.

"Oh, shit!" said Hazard, quietly. It wasn't just present company, either. If this new kind of life was real, and really was akin to a virus, then Steve Pearlman might be carrying an unobtrusive infection too…not to mention Claire Croly and Adrian Stimpson's chilled body, probably still awaiting postmortem because it was the weekend and the medical examiner wasn't on duty….

But that was ridiculous alarmism. He was quick to add: "But what happened to me was a very noticeable thing, even though I didn't understand what was happening. I think you'd know if you'd been infected already, and so would Steve. As for the possibility that I'm incubating something that might become manifest in a matter of weeks or months… well, if the entity even has a life-cycle that involves something analogous to laying eggs, insects must be its normal vectors—and as I just said, the most efficient parasites are those that do no harm to their hosts. Let's not get carried away by horror movie thinking." After a momentary pause, though, he couldn't help adding: "I could be wrong, of course—are you suggesting that I ought to quarantine myself?"

"Not if you want to avoid instant pariah status. Publicizing the fact that you've been infected by an unknown entity…well, *we* might be able to avoid horror movie thinking, but far too many people out there have seen *Alien*. If they were prepared to think that you're not crazy, they'd be expecting something loathsome by explode out of your chest at any moment. I'm presuming that it didn't explode out of your chest?"

"Seeped out of my back, apparently," Hazard said. "But the public might not appreciate the difference, given that appears to it have taken some of my blood with it. I don't feel anemic, but…well, perhaps I do need to be monitored, at least discreetly."

After another deep draught of coffee, Helen Hearne said: "You do realize, obviously, that this might eventually qualify as the discovery of the century—of the Millennium. I know they're both less than ten years old, but you know what I mean."

"It might if I can prove it," Hazard reminded her. "If not, it's just a ticket to ridicule, like seeing a yeti."

Helen Hearne looked at Margaret Dunstable. "You're already in on the conspiracy, I guess. And me too, now. But you're not thinking of taking it any further, Dr. Hazard? Even to Steve, who'd certainly believe you…as would his Fortean friend…except that with friends like that…." She left it there for a moment, before adding: "I believe it…but thousands wouldn't."

"Maybe you shouldn't," Hazard suggested. "For you, as for everyone else, at the moment, it's just my word and a couple of bloodstains that could signify almost anything. If I don't know that I'm sane, how can you?"

After a moment, she replied. "You're an entomologist, not an estate agent or a banker. If we can't trust entomologists, who can we trust?" It was a joke, but she meant it seriously. "I'm a long way down the priority ladder, but I can probably get access to the mass spec one day next week. It won't tell us much, though, as the mire is organic soup anyway, and there won't be any way to tell whether molecules in the mix belong to your entity, unless we can isolate them somehow. I'd better take samples of the stain on the doorstep, while it's still icky."

"There's a better one on the bed upstairs," Hazard told her. "We can collect a few bucketfuls of gloop from the mire tonight without any problem, but whether we can isolate any kind of entity from that is highly dubious…unless we try fishing for it."

"Fishing?" the biochemist queried.

Hazard held up his arm.

"You can't be serious."

"Yes I can. Last night, I didn't know that what I had inside me was going to come out again. If I can catch another, now that we're forewarned, I can sleep in the bath tonight. I can't be sure of catching anything, but if I do…."

Helen Hearne looked at Margaret Dunstable, but the older woman simply nodded. "It might work," she said. "It's a chance, anyhow. As John says, the most efficient parasites are the ones that don't do their hosts any harm, and if these entities did serious damage, they'd surely have been noticed before."

"And what if he fishes up one that isn't so efficient?" the biochemist countered. "And what if the nasty ones have been noticed, but simply written off as viruses. Do we really know what the agent of the Black Death was, given that people have now begun to write the rat-flea hypothesis off as a fantasy incompatible with the epidemiological evidence? But I suppose these things must be very rare…the ones capable of uploading to humans, at any rate. If the pond in Tenebrion Wood really has been isolated for two thousand years…."

"It hasn't," Hazard said. "Even if no human foot has trod there, the wood's not impermeable to small mammals, birds and moths—and let's not forget that even beetles can fly, if they need to. Not to mention that two thousand years is a blink in the eye of eternity," Hazard said. "These entities, generally speaking, must be a lot older than that."

"Millions of years, you mean?"

"The genus…or kingdom, as these things seem to be outside the normal animal/vegetable/protozoan classification, might go back billions. If their normal vector is insectile, the existing entities might have evolved in parallel. That's probably why they've never been detected—entomology is a very young science, and its history has been obsessed with pest control. Scientific investigation has always been more concerned with things that kill insects than commensals, although we do have some idea of the astonishing complexity of ant ecology. Beetles have received relatively little attention, considering God's obvious fondness for them."

"But the one that got into you is something else entirely—presumably the product of a much more recent evolution. If its kin were common parasites of any of the species we've domesticated, we'd surely know about it, individually elusive as they might be."

"I'm not sure that's true," Hazard ventured. "If these things are a different branch of the earthly life-system—if they even qualify as life at all—they must have branched at a very early stage in its evolution."

"The *urschleim*, you mean?" Margaret Dunstable put in, jumping the conclusion easily enough."

"Maybe," was all that Hazard would concede, for the moment.

"So the gap in the evolutionary schema might not be as big as you implied yesterday. There might be more relics around that we think of the chemical evolution that preceded living cells—but they haven't been recognized for what they are, because the can so easily be mistaken for decay products of organic debris…like the Bathy-whatsit you cited."

For a historian, Hazard thought, she really was very quick in the uptake—but then he criticized himself for his intellectual prejudice. Given that he was making it up as he went, floundering as he did so in misleading terminology, there was no way he could lay clam to any genuinely esoteric expertise.

"Instead of sitting around talking," Helen Hearne interjected, "We might do better to talk while strolling around the graveyard, looking for more bloodstains. We might not find any, but…."

"You're right," Hazard agreed, seizing on the suggestion as an impulsion of sorts that might serve to jerk him out of his inertia. "We really ought to take a look, just in case. No stone left unturned."

He led the way. The three of them went around Hazard's car, which had been returned to its normal parking-spot by its temporary custodian, and the entomologist opened the wrought-iron gate. He didn't feel a twinge about letting people into "his" churchyard; Margaret Dunstable had already taken a look at the illegible memorials. He paused for a moment, asking himself the absurd question of which way he would go, if he were a liquid organism.

Why, in fact, would be go anywhere? Why was the entity even on the move, when it could be still inside him as snug as a bug in a rug… with an abundant source of blood, if blood was what turned it on. At least the blood it had stolen had functioned, thus far, as a marker. If it hadn't done that….

Without making any formal agreement, the three of them fanned out. While Hazard went straight ahead, Margaret Dunstable veered left toward the church, and Helen Hearne moved to the right, along the low stone wall that marked the boundary of the churchyard on the side of the lane, toward the angle where the hedgerow commenced. Their eyes glued to the ground, they searched, suspecting that it might be futile, but unable to be certain.

How long they might have continued the search if they hadn't been interrupted, Hazard couldn't estimate—but they were interrupted, and all three of them stopped in their respective positions and turned their heads toward the far end of the lane when they heard, and then saw, the vehicle turn into it.

Yet again, it was Claire Croly's red Citroen. She hadn't had to haul his unconscious body on to the bed, but she knew that he'd hurt himself. Perhaps, like Helen Hearne, she simply wanted to make sure that he was all right. Or perhaps she was still looking for a story, and thought that she might yet get one out of Hazard, if she promised him confidentiality.

Or none of the above, he thought, as the woman got out of the car—alone, this time. He knew instantly that something was wrong. There was no mistaking the distress in the reporter's expression.

She came into the graveyard, her gaze flicking right and left to take in the biochemist and the historian. She seemed slightly glad to find them all present—but glad within the context of whatever catastrophe she had come to report.

"The wood…," she began, and then stopped a few feet away from Hazard, swallowing and groping for words, while the other two women converged on her, realizing that something bad had happened.

"What about the wood?" Hazard asked, although his stomach was already sinking, in anticipation of disaster.

"They torched it," Claire Croly managed to articulate. Last night, after we'd gone. They torched the whole bloody thing."

Hazard felt strangely numb, and dumbstruck. Helen Hearne was the one who had her priorities in order. "Is Steve all right?" she asked.

"He wasn't hurt badly," the reporter told them. "He's been taken to Newbury—the police station, not the hospital, although he has some minor burns. He phoned me from there. Even if they charge him with trespass, they'll let him go soon enough—but one of the security men was killed. They were trying to be too clever. They lit the fire first, and then went to get Steve—so that they could claim to have been rescuing him. They probably intended to claim that he'd lit a fire before falling asleep, and that it had spread, requiring them to play hero.

"That's not what they told the police though, probably because they figured that they owed him one for going back into the wood with them when they realized that one of their men was in trouble. They managed to get him out, at the cost of sustaining a few burns themselves, but he couldn't breathe. He'd presumably inhaled too much smoke. He'd got stuck in the mud, and probably panicked—and the fire spread way too rapidly. By the time the ambulance got to him—which took two hours, because it was Saturday night—he was past help. Dead on arrival in Newbury.

"I'm almost tempted to say that it served him right, but it just increases the trouble that Steve might be in. They knew he was alone, of course—they counted us is and counted us out again. He thought their bosses wouldn't pay them double time over Saturday and Sunday night just to watch us…but it never occurred to him that they might have other plans to justify the expenditure."

Hazard couldn't help forming a mental map of the wood, and the dense ring of trees surrounding the old pond. Once that ring became a circle of fire, the column of air above the mire would move upwards, drawing the flames of the blazing ring inwards centripetally—and even if the leaf litter wasn't flammable, as it might well have been, its temperature would rise drastically as it desiccated. Whatever was alive therein, or had some simulation of life, wouldn't stand the slightest chance of avoiding annihilation, if it were within a couple of feet of the surface. The conflagration must have been an insect holocaust…and perhaps worse than that for the entities he had discovered, or thought he had discovered, only a few hours before.

But they got one of the bastards, he thought. *They didn't go down without a fight.* He knew how utterly absurd it was to credit the entities in the wood with any kind of intention, but the comment seemed apposite nevertheless. All that he dared to say aloud was: "But they didn't have to do that. DEFRA was going to spray it anyway."

That seemed absurd too, and probably irrelevant. The security men knew that Steve wasn't going to give up—that he and his acolytes would try to stand off DEFRA as well as the developer's hirelings. How did they know that? Partly because Hazard had told them so himself, via Dennis Nordley. Nordley had gone back to what he had refused punctiliously to call a "council of war," but which the other people present had seen in exactly that light. And when they had received the update to Nordley's report, they had made their plan of campaign, including a preemptive strike. They hadn't wanted to wait for DEFRA; perhaps they didn't understand the significance of the Colorado beetle infestation any better than Steve Pearlman.

In the meantime, Margaret Dunstable took Claire Croly by the arm, in her curiously mock-maternal fashion, and said: "You'd better come into the house and sit down, dear."

The reporter half-turned around under the gentle pressure, but then changed her mind, and stayed where she was.

"What were you looking for when I arrived?" she asked.

"We were just taking a meditative stroll," Hazard was quick to say, while thinking that Margaret's maternal instincts had led her to make a blunder, given that Claire Croly was bound to spot the bloodstain on the doorstep, just as Helen Hearne said.

But so what? he asked himself. *It's just a bloodstain.*

For the moment, in any case, the issue wasn't going to come up. The reporter had shrugged off the helpful hand that he historian had offered her. "What are you all doing here, anyway?" she asked. "I only expected to find Dr. Hazard."

"We came to make sure that he was all right," Helen Hearne said, allowing her interlocutor to draw the false inference that she had brought Margaret Dunstable with her. "His arm seems to have made a full recovery, though."

"I was thinking about that, after we split last night," the reporter said. "It sank in a hell of a long way. Do you think that's what happened to the guy who was killed in the fire?"

"Presumably," Hazard supplied. "That can happen, when you blunder around in a mire. I presume that even you aren't going to argue in print that the goblins of the woods grabbed him in order to punish him?" *Survival of the cunning, the treacherous and the hypocritical,* he couldn't help thinking, given that the hypothesis had sprung into his own mind like a jumping flea, albeit not in earnest.

He hadn't put her off. "Two mysterious deaths in two nights is beginning to look like more than a coincidence," she said, defensively. "You were lucky it was your arm—if it had been your feet, you might not have been able to pull them out."

"You would have pulled me out, though," Hazard said. "Or Steve, at least. I wasn't in a deep hole like poor Moley. Anyway, it isn't going to happen again, is it?—not now. Has the wood been completely obliterated?"

"I think so," the reporter replied. "I haven't seen it. Steve said that it had been completely gutted, reduced to ash. There was a lot of dead wood in it, wasn't there? And it hasn't rained for a week and more. It must have gone up like a bundle of faggots—otherwise the arsonist wouldn't have been hoist by his own petard."

"Are you certain it was arson?" Margaret Dunstable asked.

"What you think?" the reporter snapped. "Would the security men have been there for any other reason? And Steve certainly didn't light a fire. He wouldn't."

"But you'll never be able to prove it, will you?" Margaret Dunstable pointed out.

"No," the reporter admitted. "Just another bloody X-file effect."

She doesn't know how right she is, Hazard thought—but he had no intention of enlightening her.

Another car turned into the lane then: a police car.

"Steve won't have said a word about us being there," Claire Croly was quick to assure them.

But the security men who weren't supposed to be there counted us all in and out again, Hazard thought. *And this time, we'd been warned about the trespass.*

They all stood there waiting, until Constable Potts came into the churchyard. He looked like a man who didn't really appreciate being called in to do extra duty on a Sunday, even if he would be drawing double pay.

"Well, this is convenient," he said, sarcastically. "A real family gathering. You've heard the news, then?"

"Yes," Hazard said, curtly.

"Are you going to charge the security firm with arson?" Claire Croly asked, boldly.

"I'm not aware of any charges pending," the constable replied, carefully, "for arson or for trespass, although I believe that Mr. Pearlman is still being questioned as to why he didn't obey a specific instruction to leave the site. I obviously didn't make myself clear enough when I spoke to you yesterday, Dr. Hazard, but for the present, as then, I'm simply here to inform you that you'll need to make a statement for the benefit of the coroner's court, as you were present shortly before the incident. It shouldn't be an inconvenience, given that you were coming into Sherfield tomorrow anyway? You can all come in together, in fact, as you seem to be inseparable at present." While certainly no expert in sarcasm, he was doing his best.

"We'll make arrangements to do that," Hazard promised.

The policeman wasn't there to conduct an interrogation, but curiosity overcame him. "Why, exactly, did you all go back?" he asked. "We know you're not econuts, and we know that you'd already advised Mr. Pearlman to give it up as a bad job, so why go back?"

Hazard shrugged. "He and Miss Croly showed me a jar full of insects," he said "I'm an entomologist. I went back to look for more." It was the truth, and nothing but the truth, even though it wasn't the whole of it.

The constable turned to Margaret Dunstable. "And you, Miss?" he asked, deliberately not addressing her as "Doctor" in order to stress her marital status, letting her know, subtly, that the police had a file on her too, or at least access to the data freshly added to the security firm's dossier.

"I just went along for the ride," the historian told him, but couldn't rest the temptation to add: "and to see if I could score. At my age, one can't afford to miss any opportunity."

"Are we under suspicion of something?" Helen Hearne put in.

"No, Miss," said the constable, again stressing the honorific slightly. "Except for the trespass, of course but I doubt that you can be charged with that, in view of the fact that the path has been opened up for general access to the farm development—the CPS wouldn't bother with it. At the end of the day, I doubt that even Mr. Pearlman will actually get to court, this time. As there's no suspicion of foul play—of any kind—the man who died last night will simply be commemorated as a hero who lost his life trying to rescue someone from a fire."

"That's bullshit," said Claire Croly.

"You should know, Miss," the policeman retorted. "You're something of an expert, after all." He was improving with practice.

"I'll come over to Sherfield tomorrow," Hazard told him. "We can get the paperwork sorted out then.

The policeman nodded. "Bring your friends," he said. He turned to go, but interrupted himself. "We know that you're hiding something," he said, "but we're prepared to assume, for now, that it isn't anything criminal. If these coincidences keep happening, though, we might begin to wonder whether the dossier that the security firm brought to us is something more than a ludicrous product of vindictive paranoia."

"Steve and Moley are the victims here," Hazard snapped. "The security man probably tripped over his own feet. They might paint him as a hero, but you know better, don't you, Mr. Potts?"

"No, I don't," the policeman countered. "And neither do you, whatever fantasies you decide to believe."

That remark, too, struck home harder than the policeman could possibly be aware of, but Hazard didn't flinch.

"He didn't even bother to ask me why I went back," Helen Hearne observed, as the policeman put his car into reverse and began to back away down the lane. "Not sufficiently important, obviously. Too young, and female."

"Don't take it to heart," Margaret Dunstable advised. "I'm sorry that I might have given him the wrong impression about you, though—he might have taken the wrong inference from my flippant remark."

"Not likely," Claire Croly put in. "He probably thought you were talking about me. People often make that assumption about me, for some reason I can't quite fathom—but I'm not going to make an effort to be more feminine just so people won't suspect I'm gay. Let them—who cares?"

Hazard hoped that he wasn't blushing visibly. He thought not; he was still wrestling mentally with the knowledge than the projected further biological investigation of Tenebrion Wood had just been torpedoed, before he'd even had a chance to formulate a semi-coherent plan. He didn't have to interrogate Margaret Dunstable and Helen Hearne to feel sure that their search of the churchyard had been as fruitless as his own. They were hunting the undetectable, far more elusive than the most recalcitrant of wild geese. All he had left was fuel for fantasy.

Without any further negotiation, they made their way back to the house. Claire Croly saw the brown bloodstain on the doorstep, but didn't make any comment on it or ask whose blood it was. Even to a reporter on the staff of the *Fortean Times*, it didn't seem sufficiently out of the ordinary to raise any hackles.

This time, Margaret Dunstable made a pot of tea. She presumably had a notion of propriety that relegated coffee to breakfast and after dinner.

"I'm still going to write the article about the wood, though," Claire Croly asserted, pugnaciously. "I'll have to be careful talking about the causes of the fire, to avoid any libelous suggestion, but the fact of it adds another dimension. It can't do Steve any good now, of course, but I was never in it just to help Steve mount a publicity campaign. I won't mention any of you, though—not by name, at any rate."

"Thanks," said Hazard, absent-mindedly.

"But you won't mind if I consult you again, if it seems that your expertise might be relevant?" the reporter added, hopefully.

"I think, on the whole, I'd rather you didn't," Hazard said. "Meaning no offense, but it really couldn't do my reputation any good to be a consultant for *Fortean Times*, however discreetly."

"I don't mind, dear," said Margaret Dunstable, and sighed before adding. "And don't look at me like that—I know you're not gay. You asked me whether you could talk to me, remember?"

Claire Croly blushed. "Yes I did," she said. "And yes, I'll certainly get in touch."

"Sometimes," Helen Hearne observed, "I feel as if I simply don't exist—or as if I were just a damp patch on the carpet."

"It's not that," the reporter hastened to assure her. "It's just that... well the two things you can't put into articles aimed at the general public are equations and chemical formulae. The readers just switch off. Biochemistry is fascinating, in scientific terms, but it's not really something I can use. And anyway, I knew you'd say exactly what Dr. Hazard said."

"It's fine," Helen Hearne assured her. "It was just a joke. And you're absolutely right, about everything."

"Not everything," said the reporter, regretfully. "There was something weird about that wood, though. I know you're not going to agree, even though you saw that jar full of insects, and it was enough to being you back again, but even though there weren't nearly as many when you came back, the place really was peculiar in some way. I don't say that it was goblins, or night-spirits, whatever the hell they're supposed to be, but there was definitely something weird about it. And now it's gone—burned down by some stroppy developer who just wanted to get rid of the Last Ditch Brigade and build his road in peace. You have to admit, don't you, that Steve's right—that's the way they think, and they'll just keep right on destroying things, without a thought for any other concerns, in the name of progress. It's a bloody shame. If the wood *had* been trying to get its own back on the bastards who burned it down, you couldn't blame it, could you? It was in the Domesday Book, for God's sake—really old."

"But you can't argue that the wood-spirits were taking revenge in your article, can you?" Margaret Constable said, mildly. "Even in the *Fortean Times*, you have to be careful not to take the fantasy too far in the wrong direction."

"You do if you don't want your copy to be cut," the reporter admitted. "But one way or another, that wood was haunted. I could feel it, and I don't care if you think that makes me crazy."

Even Hazard took the trouble to assure her that he didn't think that she was crazy, but she didn't believe him. She couldn't. He was a scientist, after all. She knew that he couldn't possibly have any sympathy for feelings of that sort.

"I don't suppose you've got any ghosts here?" she said, making conversation as she sipped her tea. "Old vicarage, churchyard full of graves with illegible inscriptions, church on the brink of collapse—it's a promising location. But you wouldn't tell me if you had would you? Bad for your image."

"Jenny thought the graveyard was haunted," Hazard admitted. "She didn't think she would when we moved out here, because she was completely confident in her own skepticism, but she underestimated the force of her impressions. The nocturnal silence worked on her nerves, and even though she knew that the tiny lights wandering among the graves were just *Lampyridae*, knowing it just wasn't enough to prevent them making her think of the souls of the dead, lost and adrift in the darkness of eternity. And in spite of all the reasons she actually gave, and the sly suspicion others have voiced that she must have been having it off with somebody else and left me for him, I think it was because she was haunted—subjectively rather than objectively, but haunted nevertheless. It's nothing you can make a story out of, though, any more than you can make a story about your own sensations in the darkling wood. There's no drama, no punch-line….just insects, misconstrued by superstitious senses."

Claire Croly looked slightly uncomfortable. "Maybe I'll track down your ex and get her side of the story," she said.

"She won't admit it," Hazard said, confidently. "Few people ever do, for fear of being thought crazy—as you said yourself, just now. It's a matter of natural selection in action—the survival of the hypocritical."

X

When Claire Croly's red Saxo had backed out of the lane and vanished from sight, there was an audible sigh of relief as the three conspirators felt free to talk again.

"What now?" asked Margaret Dunstable. "I'm assuming that we don't just give up?"

"Hardly," said Hazard. "Even if the wood is a total loss, I've made a discovery. If these things exist, they must exist elsewhere—but I'm not giving up on the wood just yet. I want to see how bad the damage is. Even if the surface of the clearing will have been carbonized, it will probably only be sterilized to a depth of a few inches—a foot at the most. The pond, when it was a pond, must have been much deeper than that, and if I dig down deep enough, I can still reach the anomalous mire. I can't guarantee that there'll be anything recoverable from it, but it's worth a try. You don't have to come, of course."

"Don't be ridiculous," said the historian. "When?"

"No time like the present. I can drop you off on the way, Helen, if you have other things to do, or if you want out. We're already on the police radar, and we will be trespassing, technically, in spite of what Constable Potts said about the opening of the road to the farm having created an implicit right of general access."

"Have you got a decent spade—and something to collect samples in?" was the biochemist's only reply.

Hazard did have a decent garden spade, and it didn't take him long to root out a few glass jars of various sizes; he hadn't been to the bottle bank for weeks."

This time, Hazard was perfectly able to drive, so they reverted to the original seating arrangements.

"I'm still trying to get my head around the idea of liquid life," Margaret Dunstable observed, as they pulled on to the road. "It's something that it never occurred to me to think about before. Especially liquid life that can just soak through the skin of solid organisms, to plunder their entrails…however discreetly."

"We mustn't get carried away with speculation," Hazard said, with a caution that he didn't really feel. "Maybe *liquid life* is an inappropriate term. What we're dealing with here is outside ordinary categories; that's why it's so difficult to get our heads around it. The way I'm conceptualizing it, such things ought to be fairly common, but they're obviously not. They're rare…it's still possible that they really are localized to the pond and its surroundings, but even if they're not, there must be something special about Tenebrion Wood that has created that strange mire, and it can't simply be the fact that the wood has isolated the pond from human contact for a long time."

"Have you considered the extraterrestrial hypothesis?" Helen Hearne asked, from the back seat.

"Yes, but I don't like it," said Hazard. "It doesn't really add anything. It's just an excuse for not looking for an explanation—the next best thing to dismissing the phenomenon as supernatural."

"But if it really did seep through your skin and then seep out again, go downstairs and make a bee-line for the graveyard, then it's definitely alive," Helen Hearne insisted, "and if it doesn't fit into the pattern of earthly life as we know it…I'm not saying that I believe it, just that it can't be rejected out of hand."

"We're biologists," Hazard reminded her. "Our first move ought to be to find a way of fitting it into the pattern of earthly life, even if we have to expend the pattern a little. We know the pattern is incomplete, because of the lack of a chemical ladder leading to the first cellular organisms—the primitive cyanobacteria. Maybe the gap isn't as big as we thought, but we've just been following the Huxley precedent, and dismissing any *urschleim* that does turn up as a product of organic decay rather than a precursor."

"But Huxley was right about *Bathybius*—didn't he work out how the decay had occurred?"

"You mean that he concocted a story as to how it might have occurred, and then found similar substances in rotting vegetable matter. The thing that got into me was in rotten vegetable matter too—maybe it was a product of decay, and maybe, if we'd managed to isolate it and subject it to chemical analysis, we'd have killed it and caused it to degenerate—just another instance of the act of observation affecting the properties of the observed."

"You do realize that you're talking about spontaneous generation?" the biochemist said.

"Of course I do. Spontanous generation is one of the great discredited theories: a universally-acknowledged scholarly fantasy, thanks to Pasteur—except that Pasteur's demonstration was a farcical publicity stunt, and his real reason for putting it on was that he was trying to discredit Darwin's theory of evolution, the logic of which entails some kind of spontaneous generation at its starting-point. It's just an item of faith that the spontaneous generation that gave rise to earthly life only happened once in the distant past, and that all extant living organisms have a single common ancestor. The fact that they're all related might just mean that they follow the same pattern of chemical evolution—but it might have happened many times in the past, and might, in fact, still be happening. Not everywhere, certainly, and probably mostly in mud at the bottom of the sea, and maybe not all the time—but it's certainly not inconceivable that it can happen in numerous different circumstances, in various combinations. And it's conceivable, too, that such processes can produce other things than elementary cyanobacteria."

"Yes, but colloidal quasiviruses? Vampiric colliodal quasiviruses big enough to leave that stain on your doorstep?"

Hazard didn't like the term *quasiviruses* any better than the others that had been invoked for want of anything better, but he let it pass. "It's not a vampire," he said. "I shouldn't have suggested that it was—sloppy thinking and letting my mouth run away with it. In a way, it's the reverse of a vampire."

"What do you mean?"

"It—or they—didn't want the hemoglobin, evidently. It, or they, ex-creted that, presumably having dissolved it along with other materials."

"Such as what?"

"Principally metabolizable body fat, I suspect. The fact that I lost about a stone when it made its exit obviously doesn't mean that the entity weighed a stone before it oozed into me, and I suspect that much of the excess that it took aboard while it was inside me was weight I'd recently put on. I suspect that what happened to me was more akin to discreet liposuction than blood donation. The blood was probably only there be-cause body fat is deposited around capillaries—have you ever seen the blood-soaked muck that liposuction pulls out of people?"

"If that's so," said Margaret Dunstable, "and if you can work out how the trick was done, you can probably make a fortune out of the practical applications: cosmetic surgery without cutting, with inbuilt lo-cal anesthetics."

"I'll be sure to put all our names on the patent application," said Hazard, dryly. "That way, we'll all get rich when we sell it on."

"Too late for me," the historian observed. "Even if you can dig some-thing out of the pond and make rapid headway with the investigation, it will take years to get the process through the field trials and safety tests. I could volunteer for the trials, I suppose—but no amount of slimming down is going to turn back the clock forty years, is it? Still, I appreciate the offer, given that I'm essentially a passenger, and you two will be doing all the real work."

The traffic was expectably light, and they made it to the lay-by in record time.

As Steve Pearlman had told Claire Croly, the fire had reduced Tenebrion Wood to a carpet of ash, with a few bristling black spikes where the charred remains of the sturdiest saplings had retained a vestige of verticality. The tracks along the lane to the hamlet suggested that a fire appliance had eventually made its way out to the blaze, as well as the ambulance that had collected the dead security man, but there was no evidence that any extensive fire-fighting had been done. The firemen had simply let the wood burn out, while presumably monitoring the situation to make sure that the blaze didn't spread across the fields. The appliance was long gone, along with the body and the security men. The area hadn't been taped off, and no one had been left to guard it. It wasn't a crime scene—and it was Sunday, after all.

Killing the fire as it began to make its way through the grass in the fields around the wood couldn't have been difficult, given that the wind-tunnel created by the fire had drawn the flames inwards toward the clearing and there had been no significant external breeze. The blaze must have been easy to contain and confine.

The ash-carpet was still hot in places, especially where it was more than ankle deep, but there was no danger of the soles of Hazard's rubber boots melting as he negotiated a path to the clearing. Margaret Dunstable's shoes protected her feet well enough, although she had to be careful where she put her feet, and Hazard suspected that no amount of brushing was going to return them to their original shade of brown once they were out of the ex-wood.

As Hazard had anticipated, the surface layer of the clearing had been badly seared, and there was now a thick layer of soot and ash over the circular space. The stink was unpleasant, but not unbearable.

The hole that Adrian Stimpson had dug in the middle of the clearing was still there, although the half-rampart he'd built had shriveled considerably, much of the organic litter constituting it having burned. Calcined debris had accumulated in the pit. Hazard knew that he was going to get absolutely filthy, but he had dressed for the occasion. He lowered himself into the hole, and started shoveling out the loose muck that had accumulated during the fire.

He worked rapidly, figuring that it wouldn't take him long to get down to uncharred soil. He remained on his guard, ready to pull himself out of the hole—leaving his boots behind, if necessary—if the mire started to suck him down.

His companions stood by, ready to help with that if need be; although neither of them was unusually sturdy, they had already demonstrated that they could lift his weight, working in association.

Hazard had been toiling away for a quarter of an hour, concentrating fiercely, when an angry voice demanded: "What the hell do you people think you're doing?"

Margaret Dunstable and Helen Hearne had had their backs to the direction from which the red-faced newcomer was arriving—the direction of the revamped dwellings that had previously been the farm buildings—so they were as surprised as Hazard.

Hazard weighed the man up as he covered the last twenty yards separating him from the intruders, crunching his way through the debris of saplings that were still bristling the black earth. He was big, a good four inches taller than Hazard, and much of the extra broadness looked like muscle, but Hazard decided that the best policy was not to allow the newcomer's obvious aggression to intimidate him. He wasn't, in any case, in a timid mood.

"Digging a hole," he announced, blandly.

Margaret Dunstable and Helen Hearne moved apart, allowing the big man to reach the edge of the excavation, where he towered above Hazard, chest deep in the black hole.

"You're trespassing! This is private property."

"And you aren't?" Hazard queried, already anticipating what the answer would be.

"I own the land," the other declared, ominously. "And I want you off it, right now. Who the hell are you, anyhow?"

"John Hazard—I'm a biologist. Dr. Nordley talked to me on Friday; he must have mentioned my name to you while you were holding the meeting at which you planned to torch the wood—a plan that seems to have cost one of your employees his life, rather than the intended victims."

Hazard wasn't surprised that the speech increased the Evil Developer's wrath by a further order of magnitude, but he was surprised by the way the increase seemed to give his antagonist sudden pause. Something he had said seemed to have upset the landowner very considerably, and he didn't think that it was the unjustified accusation of attempted murder.

"What did that bastard Nordley tell you?" demanded the property speculator. "He signed a confidentiality agreement! I'll have his guts for bloody garters!"

Hazard immediately tried to recall the details of his brief encounter with Dennis Nordley. He was virtually certain that the ecologist hadn't told him anything at all, except for venturing the bare hypothesis that the clearing was a dried-up pond, which could hardly be considered prejudicial in any way to his employer. On the other hand, the mere fact that the property developer thought that there was something prejudicial that Nordley *might* have told him spoke volumes, in its own way. The man from Imperial had been hired to pre-empt Steve Pearlman's anticipated attempt to find something on the site that might provide grounds for defending it on the grounds that it was a Site of Special Scientific Interest, as he had tried to do with Egypt Mill, but Nordley had implied very strongly that he hadn't found any such thing. What else, then, could he have found that alarmed his employer?

Then everything clicked into place, and Hazard abruptly realized what it was that Nordley had observed, and why it was important. Clearly, Nordley had reported it to his employer, and had explained the implications, but unlike the Colorado beetles, which he had been required to report by law, he couldn't reveal his other conclusion to anyone because of the confidentiality agreement he's signed. Hazard knew the guess was correct because it provided an explanation of why the developer had decided to torch the wood, instead of simply waiting for DEFRA to spray the site with insecticide. It had been a belated attempt to cover up the evidence—and a futile one, given that Hazard was now standing in Moley's hole, digging down into the anomalous earth.

The landowner, of course, had no idea why he was doing that—but he probably had every reason not to want him to do it.

"As a matter of fact, Dr. Nordley didn't tell me anything," Hazard said, evenly. "He didn't have to. I'm a biologist—it's not my specialism, but it really didn't need a plant ecologist to figure it out. It didn't even need Steve Pearlman to persuade someone like me to come out and look, really. Sooner or later, the problem would have become manifest, and hoping that you could simply bury the evidence in ash was wildly optimistic. Sending in a JCB to level the debris of site wouldn't have worked, even if you'd done it this morning instead of waiting until tomorrow. Any possibility that there was that you'd be allowed to build houses along this path, even with a fast-tracked planning application, disappeared as soon as Nordley's helpers had hacked a way through to the clearing."

"If he'd kept quiet...." The landowner began, but didn't finish the sentence.

"Is that really what you thought?" Hazard countered. "You really thought that the problem would simply disappear if no one pointed at it any shouted: *Danger!* Nordley must have told you that, even in the most optimistic estimate, you could only buy a little time."

The expression of the property developer's overwrought face told Hazard that that was exactly the point. The developer had been trying to buy time. And he might have bought a little—months, even, perhaps time enough to protect his financial situation, if Hazard hadn't come back to the site, and hadn't had a reason to resume investigations there.

"Well," said Hazard, "you haven't bought any, Mr. Whatever-your-name-is. I don't suppose the failure of a piddling little project like this will bankrupt you, but I wouldn't be at all surprised if the purchasers you have lined up for the conversions you've already completed will not only refuse to complete but will probably go to court to reclaim their deposits."

He paused, wondering momentarily whether the developer might try to bribe him, but he'd made his own speech too well. Obviously, Nordley hadn't been able to talk sense into the moron, but Hazard had only needed three minutes to convince him that the game was up. As soon as he had calmed down, he would start making a new set of contingency plans.

"Take the hit and chalk it up to experience," Hazard advised, feeling rather pleased with himself. "Without Steve Pearlman's intervention, the whole truth might have taken years to come out, but it was always bound to become manifest eventually, and the repercussions would have been worse if people were actually living on the site. Nordley must have told you that. You might have been able to gag him, but sooner or later, it would have come out. Maybe you were hoping that you might be able to make a quick killing and get the hell out before the shit hit the fan, but I doubt that it was possible, let alone ethical."

"Just get the hell off my land!" repeated the landowner.

Hazard steeled himself, although he felt surprisingly confident.

"No," he said. "There's something I need to do that has nothing to do with your stupid planning applications: something far more important—at least to me. You can try and throw me off your land by means of assault and battery if you want to, but it will only make the story bigger, when the papers publish details of Moley's death and the death of your security man tomorrow. If I get added to the list of your victims, you can be damn sure that the motive for your actions will be right there in the headline. So, if you're not going to attack me physically, I'd be obliged if you'd go away and let me get on with it."

The developer's fury was still at the apoplectic level, but Hazard judged that even if he hadn't glanced to his left and right at the two patient witnesses, he wouldn't have lost his temper completely. The developer knew that Hazard knew what he had been desperately but hopelessly trying to conceal ever since he had heard Dennis Nordley's judgment on the mysterious clearing in a middle of his wood—the previously-inaccessible clearing that no human foot had trod or centuries. The developer probably didn't know that he was the one who had just drawn Hazard's attention to the significance of the inference to which he had previously given little thought, but Hazard would have realized its importance soon enough, long before the developer could wangle his way through the planning regulations to get permission to build more houses on the site.

"In fact," Hazard added, meditatively, "there's actually no point in your widening the road now, is there? All you've achieved by burning the wood is to deny Steve Pearlman the satisfaction of saving it—and knowing Steve, I think he'll count it as a victory anyway, when I explain to him exactly why you're up shit creek without a paddle. Now, as I say, I'm still hoping to save something from the wreckage of your environmental vandalism, so unless you want the headlines in next week's papers to turn seriously nasty, I'd be grateful if you'd just fuck off and die, and let me trespass in peace."

The expressions on the faces of his two companions had now gone past mere astonishment, and were bordering on horror. They didn't think that the property developer would take that lying down. Nor did he—but Hazard had been right to gauge that he had sufficient self-control to contain his wrath, at least to prevent him from launching a physical attack upon his insulter. He was a businessman, after all, an expert in cunning, treachery and hypocrisy, a survivor rather than a mere brute.

"You haven't heard the last of this, Hazard!" the businessman threatened. It was probably not an entirely empty threat, but it wasn't sufficiently weighty to cause Hazard any undue concern.

"Nor have you," he pointed out. "And there's a strong possibility that any mud you try to sling at me will simply rebound."

With that, Hazard turned his back on the enraged property-developer and resumed digging.

"Now that," said Margaret Dunstable, when the landowner had gone, "was truly impressive. Meaning no offense, but I would never have guessed that you had it in you."

"Nor would I," Hazard confessed. "I got carried away when I suddenly realized what he was so upset about. If I hadn't been so preoccupied with beetles and exotic invasive entities, I'd have realized long ago, but when you're looking intently in one place, it's surprisingly easy to overlook the obvious sitting alongside it."

"At the risk of seeming foolish," said the historian, "what obvious thing am I overlooking?"

"I thought Nordley was testing my scientific credentials when he drew out what I'd deduced about the pond, but he was just checking to make sure that I'd reached the same conclusion he had," Hazard explained. "He knew where that train of thought would lead me, when I got around to following it—I've just been a bit slow on the uptake because I had other issues on my mind. He knew that once I'd elaborated the pond hypothesis slightly, that he wouldn't have to think about breaking his confidentiality agreement to turn whistleblower. The dried-up pond is a blatant symptom of a significant disruption of the local water table. I've already mentioned pesticide residues a couple times, without taking note of the full significance of the fact that if the local water-table has been polluted, and if that fact is published loudly enough, there's no way that the developer is going to get planning permission to do any more building here. Steve mentioned the possibility too, seemingly without realizing that it was better dynamite than the tactics he's used before at Egypt Mill. In purely legalistic terms, it's a clincher far more powerful than any bullshit about special scientific interest, even though you and I know that the latter case is far more important in the greater scheme of things."

"Why didn't Steve think of it?" Helen Hearne asked.

"He didn't realize that the matter could be properly investigated, for once, and the claim proven. The entire area looks run down, but that could be due to simple soil exhaustion. The dead pond and the affected soil elsewhere in the wood are the only *prima facie* evidence of something nasty going on below. Steve would probably have caught on, even without my help, if the coroner inquiring into Moley's death had started asking serious questions about the anomalous nature of the soil, but given that there was no indication of foul play, that procedure might just have been a rubber stamp job. The guy with the red face thought that he still had a chance of literally burying the problem, and keeping it underground for months—maybe years…but even if I hadn't had a reason to come back and dig, I'd have been able to steer Steve in the right direction for his next step."

Helen Hearne already had her phone in her hand, thumbing what was presumably Steve Pearlman's number. She didn't get through immediately, though, and had to leave a message. Presumably, the heroic ecowarrior was still being questioned at the police station.

"So the pending planning applications will be stalled even by the mere suggestion that the ground-water is polluted?" Margaret Dunstable queried, dubiously.

"It's a doubly sensitive issue" Hazard told her. "Granting such applications is always a political risk—and anxiety about pollution caused be pesticide residues is running high at present. Usually, there's no real evidence to support such suggestions, because there's no chain of evidence, but we're standing on a literal conduit from the surface down to what was once a vigorous spring feeding water to a pond, but is now a source of gradual organic seepage—maybe a stimulus to exotic evolution, from my viewpoint, but certainly an apparent health hazard from the viewpoint of the people who have bought those nice new cottages over there. When those people find out that they'll be moving on to land sitting on top of a polluted water table, their enthusiasm for the country idyll is likely to wane rapidly. As I pointed out to the angry guy, they'll probably want their deposits back, and he won't be able to get rid of the properties he's already built without dropping the price drastically."

"So he was hoping to stop them finding out, at least until the purchases were completed," the historian concluded. "He thought that if he burned the wood and got rid of Mr. Pearlman's people immediately, he'd be able to move in earth-moving equipment to cover up the evidence, literally."

"That's the way it looks," Hazard confirmed. "It was probably foolish, but the temptation is understandable. Further effects of the pollution will show up over time, and the mere fact that he commissioned Nordley's report, even if Nordley never says a word and he burns the document itself, will always be hanging over his head, to testify that he knew about the problem. You can understand, though, why he threw a fit when he saw me digging here. He doesn't know that what I'm digging for is far more important than his poxy financial problems. He thought I was digging for evidence of the pollution."

"I should have realized that myself," said Helen Hearne, presumably meaning the importance of the pollution of the water table. "If I'd told Steve yesterday, when he raised the possibility…."

"It wouldn't have made any difference," Hazard reassured her. "That crazy bastard had already decided on the scorched earth policy. If the pollutants did play some role in stimulating the development of the liquid entities—which is not inconceivable, even if it does sound like something out of a superhero comic—that's all the more reason for trying to figure out the chemistry of what's happening down there. Fundamentally, though, it ought to be something that goes on in mires and peat-bogs routinely, even without the intervention of exotic man-made organic compounds. Either way, we need to fill these bottles and jars and hope that we can dig out something detectable."

Having said that, he resumed digging, at the same furious pace as before, piling up heaps of shifted earth round the rim of the hole, just as Moley had, while keeping an uneasy eye on the walls for any danger of collapse.

In the meantime, Helen Hearne's phone buzzed, as Steve Pearlman replied belatedly to the message she'd left on his voicemail, and she automatically moved away across the ashy surface, although she didn't have anything to say to the ecowarrior that her companions didn't already know.

"He's been released," she reported, when she had concluded the call. "They haven't charged him. They warned him that the landowner might bring a civil charge for trespass, but he wasn't worried about that even before I told him that the landowner probably won't even go ahead with widening the road now that he can foresee the trouble lurking ahead. He's upset about the wood, of course, but cock-a-hoop about the complications."

That was hardly news. Hazard knew that Pearlman had never really cared about the wood and its biological and historical significance; those issues had just been cards to play in his ongoing game.

Hazard didn't reach liquid mud, but he was soon digging into much softer earth, with the strange, sticky texture of which Moley had complained two days before. He kept digging until he had reached a depth of more than six feet, and then he began filling the specimen bottles, which the three of them had brought in several plastic bags.

Once the jars were full, and stowed in the plastic bags again, Hazard jammed his left hand into the mire, as deeply as it would go—but nothing happened, and he drew it out again after a couple of minutes, feeling slightly foolish. He wiped it as clean as he could, and looked up at his two companions, who were watching him tolerantly. He wasn't about to stand there like a patient angler for hours on end, without a bite. That really would give him every appearance of insanity.

The substance he'd piled into the jars was so very unprepossessing that Hazard found it difficult to believe that it contained anything potentially capable of adding a new dimension to biological understanding, but he had set his course, and there was no turning back now. If he had to spend the rest of his life searching in vain for a secret that he had once glimpsed, and which had slipped away from him, so be it. The prize was worth the effort, and not because it might conceivably be worth millions to the slimming industry.

XI

By the time they got back to town, it was long past lunchtime. Steve dropped Margaret Dunstable and Helen Hearne at their respective residences so that they could clean up and change their dirty clothes, which had suffered considerably from the excursion, as had his car, which would need a very thorough internal clean-up. He made arrangements with his co-conspirators to pick them up again so that the three of them could grab a pizza together and he and Helen could map out some kind of general research plan.

"In the meantime," Hazard said, "I'm going to pick up some elementary equipment from the lab, and set up a work facility at the vicarage—nothing fancy, though." Addressing the historian, he explained: "I'll have to rely on Helen to do the basic analytical work using her departmental equipment, but at least I'll have a microscope, and some Petri dishes in which to incubate cultures."

"Will you go back to the site again?" the older woman asked.

"Probably. DEFRA will still spray, of course, to make sure that the Colorado beetles are extinct, but it's not necessarily the case that their spraying will destroy any life-forms lurking at the bottom of the ex-pond. I might not be the only one investigating, of course, if anyone else's imagination is promoted by the circumstances of Moley's death, but that's okay—the more the merrier. It's the truth I'm after, not the glory."

Over dinner, Hazard and Helen Hearne tried to work out a plan of procedure, discussing possible avenues of inquiry, and precautions that needed to taken in preserving and protecting their specimens. She seemed unworried by the possibility that it might all be a colossal waste of time, although she did insist that she would need to give her first priority to writing up her thesis.

"That's all right," Hazard told her. "Obviously, I'll keep taking census of my experimental *Tribolium* populations, following the set routine. We both have to secure the career we have before gambling our time at long odds on the possibility of finding a better one."

The discussion was still going on when Hazard drove all three of them back to the vicarage, ostensibly to inspect the preparations he'd made before taking them home. In fact, it was the momentum of the situation that was making them a trifle reluctant to part company. They had formed a bond of sorts, which was still sufficiently new to seem tight.

The inspection of his preparations never happened, however. That poor excuse for a gathering was discarded as soon as they turned into the lane leading to the church and saw a red Citroen Saxo parked outside the house. Claire Croly and Steve Pearlman were sitting on the wall of the churchyard, patiently waiting for Hazard to come home. Clearly, they hadn't bothered to phone when they arrived, in order to discover where Hazard was. He inferred that they had wanted to surprise him. He was duly surprised.

The ecowarrior didn't seem astonished to find the entomologist still in company with Margaret Dunstable and Helen Hearne.

"I knew you three were up to something," he said, as soon they got out of the car. "When Helen told me that you'd gone back to the burnt-out wood, I knew that you must have found something there without letting on. Well, don't worry about it—you have my blessing, whatever it is. We didn't save the wood, but if we've thrown a spanner in the works of the juggernaut of development, we're entitled to call it a draw, which isn't a bad result in these hard times. I wanted to thank you for that, so I got Claire to drive me out here. I thought you'd be home, Doc—I didn't realize that your social life had stepped up a gear."

"And it's all due to you, for bringing us together," Hazard commented, emphasizing the irony in his tone.

"Claire figured out that you were up to something too," Pearlman continued breezily, "after finding you as thick as thieves this morning—but she isn't going to harass you about it." He held up a bottle of wine—cheap Australian red, Hazard guessed. "I don't really know whether this is to celebrate the developer's defeat or to mourn the passing of the darkling wood, but I figured that we were entitled to clink glasses either way…if only because, as you say, it was me that brought the three of you together for whatever unholy partnership you've decided to form."

"Mind you," Claire Croly put in, "I'll be deeply disappointed if you don't let me in on whatever you found once you're ready to go public. I've done my bit, after all—if it hadn't been for me bringing those beetles out here, you wouldn't have gone back there yesterday, would you, Dr. Hazard?"

Hazard shook his head, as if to deny it, but conceded privately that he probably wouldn't have. He didn't bother denying that he was "up to something," nor did he bother to try to explain that it might take him years to produce anything sufficiently substantial to "go public," if he ever did. In the meantime he had no intention of giving *Fortean Times* a story of which its pages would probably make a typical flight of wild fancy, given that it would be reported without too much inconvenient biochemistry or speculative restraint.

They all went into the house together, where Steve insisted on opening the wine and forcing them to celebrate whatever it was that they were celebrating. In spite of their promise of non-harassment, however, Steve Pearlman and Claire Croly were both curious to know what Hazard was "up to," and they tacitly adopted a policy of divide and conquer. While Steve worked on Helen Hearne, maneuvering her into a corner, Claire Croly tried to isolate Hazard, presumably working on the hypothesis that a little innocent flirtation might be a useful lever—but Margaret Dunstable wasn't about to be left sitting in an armchair like a fifth wheel relegated to the trunk of a car; she stuck with Hazard and the reporter.

"I know that it's something to do with the beetles," the reporter told Hazard, "and something to do with why your arm went numb. I know it doesn't seem very newsy, but you never know. I promise I won't mention your name."

"As soon as I have anything *newsy*," Hazard assured her, insincerely "I'll be certain to let you know—even before I sent a note to the *British Journal of Entomology*."

Changing tactics, the young woman turned to the historian, perhaps thinking that fluttering eyelashes might work on her too. "It must be something that would interest a much wider public than scientific specialists," she observed, "since you're an expert of ancient British history."

"And Medieval," the older woman pointed out. "Not to mention scholarly fantasies—you and I have far more in common than either of us might care to think, my dear. But I'm not really interested in what Dr. Hazard might find in all that yucky soil—you should see what it's done to my shoes. I'm just trying to get into Helen's knickers."

Claire Croly blushed, and laughed, but obviously didn't find the suggestion implausible.

"No need to be jealous, dear," sad the historian, keeping a perfectly straight face. "You can have Dr. Hazard; I've no intention of competing with you there. Tread carefully, though—he hasn't got over his wife yet."

It as obviously on the tip of the reporter's tongue to blurt out that she had no interest of that sort in Hazard, but she stopped herself in time, remembering that she was being teased. She might have been tempted momentarily to respond in kind by insisting, falsely, that it was Margaret Dunstable in whom she was interested, but that would have been a step too far, and she had already taken note of the older woman's alacrity with a sharp comeback. Instead, she changed tack again.

"Steve and I took a walk through your graveyard," she said, "trying to figure out what you were looking for earlier. It really is an interesting place—as neglected and isolated, in its way, as Tenebrion Wood."

"It's not in the Domesday Book," Hazard observed. "The church was built much later than that. And the peasants who worshipped there, and were buried in its grounds, made no impact at all on history or the generic heritage of humankind. They were ephemera, in effect. They didn't even leave a single ghost behind."

"That's not what your wife thought, apparently." The reporter knew that it was a sore point, but she was retaliating to the provocation of Margaret Dunstable's subtle gibes.

"It's easy enough for people to conjure up imaginary night-spirits," Hazard told her. "Indeed, there are times and circumstances in which people can't help it. Oversensitivity causes them to transform the slightest of signals—the flight of a bat, the clicking of a death-watch beetle, or the glimmer of a firefly, into something much stranger than it really is. And when other people attempt to persuade them that it's just a product of their imagination, they construe it as an insult to their intelligence, and become resentful—and the conviction is tempered and hardened by the suspicion itself. That's how ghosts are manufactured, Miss Croly, as well as all the other phenomena in which Forteans are so interested, whether they're cryptozoological, extraterrestrial or paranormal. But because we're all vulnerable to the syndrome, we're also fascinated by it. The truth is dull, while scholarly fantasies are colorful. That's why your magazine has such a large circulation, while hardly anyone reads the *British Journal of Entomology*, including the subscribers."

"That doesn't mean that there isn't a story in your haunted churchyard," the dutiful Fortean pointed out.

"Probably not," Hazard agreed. "I'll give you Jenny's new address, if you like. Good luck with getting her to talk about it, though, especially if you het her know that I put you on to her—and if she picks up any cutlery, duck. She always aims for the eyes."

Claire Croly looked him in the face, but not to search for evidence of scars. "I understand people's reluctance to talk about these things," she told him, meaning his reluctance rather than Jenny's, "but bear in mind that I'm one of the few people guaranteed to take you seriously….far more so, I suspect, than someone like Dr. Dunstable."

"Ouch," said the historian, sarcastically. "You really know how to hurt a person, don't you? Try to remember that I'm just a vulnerable old lady, will you?"

The reporter shook her head, affecting weariness, in order to signal that she wasn't fooled. Then she turned to look out of the window at the fading twilight, as if to search the churchyard across the lane of evidence of restless specters emerging from their graves to greet the impending darkness....

Then, abruptly, she ran out of the room and turned right, toward the front door.

"Was it something I said?" Margaret Dunstable asked, mockingly.

"No," said Hazard, having followed the direction of the younger woman's. "No, it wasn't."

And he too set off for the front door, at a run.

Within a minute, they were all outside, having exited the garden and crossed the lane, dodging round the Mondeo and the Saxo. At the wall of the churchyard, however, they paused. No one opened the wrought-iron gate to go in. They simply stood and watched.

As the last of the twilight faded discreetly away into the sky, where the stars were already twinkling between slowly-drifting wisps of fleecy cumulus cloud, clouds of a different kind were forming closer to the earth, above the churchyard: clouds of gray moths, swirling in the still air, becoming every more compact. And below those living clouds, the entire churchyard was lighting up, moment by moment, with a further set of twinkling stars, far, far more abundant than the fugitive glints in the sky.

There had always been *Lampyridae* in the churchyard while Hazard was living in the house, and presumably long before that, although, like the *Tenebrio* in Tenebrion Wood, they were really invaders from the south, migrants who had come to Britain when the temperature had become milder after the little ice age of the seventeenth century. They were not given to synchronization of their blinking, like some of the bugs in the Far East and North America, nor were they harassed by *Photinus* species that imitated firefly blinks in order to attract the males of innocuous species and eat them. They just lived in the churchyard, as quietly and unspectacularly as he lived in the house, and even though they had been sufficiently evident to disturb Jenny and feed her fantasies, they had never been present in large numbers.

Until now.

Now there were no longer a few dozen, but thousands, perhaps hundreds of thousands, flashing away like crazy, at random.

The churchyard was lit up like a gaudy Christmas tree, flashing away as if to provoke epileptic fits in any susceptible observers—but none of the five people witnessing the event was prone to epilepsy, and they continued watching, amazed and hypnotized by the show.

It was spectacular, and also beautiful, but all John Hazard could think, to begin with, was: *It doesn't make sense. Lampyridae don't produce pheromones. They use their bioluminescence to attract mates. There's no earthly way that this many individuals could have been gathered together in next to no time. The moths, maybe—they do employ pheromones, but not the fireflies. It doesn't make sense.*

Except, of course, that it *had* to make sense somehow. It couldn't be a supernatural. There was no such thing as a supernatural phenomenon. Everything that happened was, by definition, natural—maybe not normal, in the sense of being commonplace, but natural, in the sense of having a cause. Appearances could be deceptive, but they couldn't not make sense. One way or another, it had to make sense.

The cloud and the light-show were already attracting predators: bats and nocturnal-birds. The rustling in the undergrowth also signified that the local hedgehogs had sensed a bonanza. The clouds were becoming more confused, and the phenomenon more complicated, but the show went on and on; the moths continued swirling, the beetles continued flashing.

It was magnificent, and it was unique.

Caravaggio, Hazard knew, was reputed to have used luciferase derived from crushed fireflies to prepared his canvases, to give his images a discreet quality of phosphorescence. The painter had not known, of course, that the light emitted by the beetles was a system of sexual signaling, a language of amour, but he would doubtless have been delighted to find out, not because he would have thought that the signals might work on humans as well as other fireflies, but because he would have understood the symbolism of giving his lush paintings a slight sexual glow.

The beauty of the world, Hazard thought, *is owed far more to insects than people think. They aren't intelligent, even though what fantasists call hive-minds can sometimes simulate intelligence, but the human sense of beauty isn't really a matter of intelligence either: it's a sensibility that rises from the subconscious, from inherited instincts that go back millions, or billions, of years. And it's more primitive even than the insects....maybe older, and more elementary than life itself.*

Hazard did understand, just as he imagined that Caravaggio might have understood, although he didn't suppose that his companions did, as yet. He understood that the light-show and the cloud-show that he was watching was an orgy of sorts, far more frenzied than any merely human orgy had ever been or ever could be. It was a bacchanal, a display of insanity...except that beneath and within the insanity, there had to be a kind of sanity, a logic of sorts. Obviously, in this case, it was a logic that went beyond the customary logic of routine mate attraction, of polite seduction, but nevertheless, there had to be a logic. Although his own experience had undoubtedly been polluted by the stuff of dreams, and probably still was, making it hard to know exactly where the boundary between the real and the fantastic lay, there had to be a rationale, a way in which it all made sense. That was the scientific credo, without which nothing at all could be known, or discovered.

Obviously, this marvel was the work was the entity—or the *stuff*—that had hitched a ride out of the dead pond of Tenebrion Wood inside his body, borrowing some of his metabolic reserves in the process, but spitting out the hemoglobin, because it wasn't a vampire and that sort of thing wasn't to its taste. The *stuff*—he had to be careful not to think of it as a *thing*, because that would have implied an individuality that it clearly didn't have—had been drawn to the graveyard because it had some sort of primitive sensory capacity, presumably a form of olfaction. And it had flowed into the grass of the churchyard, and spread out, as only a mobile liquid could, drawn to its ultimate insectile targets…but why? To invade them? To consume them?

While it was just a matter of *Tenebrio*, and moths, the hypothesis that that the stuff had used pheromone mimics to summon them had been plausible, but not any more. There was only one way that so many fireflies could have appeared in the space of a single day. These were no adults, summoned from elsewhere; they had been produced locally, by the mass metamorphosis of larvae.

Normally, as Hazard had earlier pointed out to Margaret Dunstable when she had accidentally hit upon a hypothesis that now seemed far more plausible than it had at the time, larvae had to go through a long pupal stage before emerging as adults—but they nevertheless had the physical capacity to metamorphose, which was presumably capable of acceleration. He knew from his own experience with *Tribolium*, in fact, that the periodicity of such phase-changes was surprisingly variable, Perhaps the imagoes produced by that accelerated metamorphosis were imperfect, but if they were fireflies, evidently, they could still flash.

But normal fireflies had to flesh discreetly, because using a method like that to attract mates carried a built in risk of attracting predators too. That, Hazard realized, might be what the *stuff* was doing, in following its built-in tropisms; perhaps it was aiming for ingestion, for being swallowed. Not that it had to be swallowed in order to make progress. It had other options, provided that its hosts could get up close and purpose with other organisms. It could simply flow from one to another, using natural local anesthetics just as mosquitoes did, to avoid provoking an instant reaction of withdrawal. It was versatile, and clever. The *stuff*, if it was a life-form, might seem primitive, by comparison with cellular organisms, but it wasn't; like them it as a product of billions of years of natural selection, of the fittest and the caring, of the cunning, the treacherous and the hypocritical. Among other capacities, it was so good at hiding that biochemistry—a science still, after all, in its infancy—had barely caught glimpses of it as yet.

Normally, obviously, the process of parasitization happened on a small scale, very discreetly, but in special circumstances, the *stuff* could accumulate, not just into droplets but whole ponds, relatively speaking— and then, when an opportunity for redistribution came up....

Liquid life, Hazard realized, had to be everywhere; it just hadn't been identified, because it melted into its background, becoming indistinguisable from the organic flesh that carried it. The evolutionary ladder connecting classified organisms with inert matter hadn't been swallowed up as completely as it seemed; it was just that the multitudinous species of *urschleim* were very hard to recognize for what they were.

Biologists were only beginning to realize that complex organisms, including humans, were actually entire worlds in their own right, populated by vast hosts of bacterial species, many of which were probably unique to a particular line of genetic descent, or even to a single individuals; and those bacteria weren't just parasites or passengers; many of them had functions within life of the whole entity, and without which the entity could not survive, unable to function biochemically, or even mentally.

Complex organisms, including human beings were more like lichens than appearances had long suggested to their scientific observers, more like colonies of symbiotes than simple individuals. And just as bioscientists had long been unaware of the roles played by bacteria in their own being, they were still unaware of an entire spectrum of other entities, which must have been among their ancestors' partners all the way back to the age of reptiles, the age of insects, and the age when life was still cofined to the sea...all the way back to the primordial sludge, when the remotest ancestors of the *stuff* had only had cyanobacteria to flow into, out of and between.

But proving it was going to be a hell of a job, even if the muck he had collected from the dead pond did turn out to contain other gargantuan aggregations of *stuff* like the one that had grabbed his arm and hitched a ride in him. He had evidence enough to convince him before his very eyes, but he knew that it was going to be an ephemeral phenomenon, and he knew that the other four people watching it were not seeing what he was seeing, and not understanding what he was understanding, because they didn't have the appropriate intellectual context into which to fit it.

He knew that he could make Helen Hearne understand, because she was a biochemist, and smart enough to follow the logic every step of the way, and he knew that Margaret Dunstable would go along with it whether she understood it fully or not, because she was a lonely, aged academic terrified by the isolation of impending retirement. He could probably explain it to Claire Croly and Steve Pearlman too, if he wanted to, and they would take his word for it even if they couldn't grasp it fully....but even the evidence of all five of them wouldn't be sufficient defense against the suspicion of the world at large that they were imagining things, jumping to conclusions and concocting scholarly fantasies. To convince anyone else, he was going to need evidence far more substantial than the word of five witnesses that hey had seen an exotic display of strange behavior by a host of months and a bizarre profusion of fireflies.

Even though the present phenomenon was unlikely to be repeated, though, he supposed that the introduction of the *stuff* into the churchyard would have long term repercussions. From now until God alone knew when, the quantity and behavior of the indigenous insect species was likely to manifest all kinds of anomalies that an entomologist, especially an expert in population dynamics, would be able to detect and track—but building an argument for the existence and evolutionary importance of a whole new class of biological entities on evidence of that sort was a task to make any intellectual Hercules blanch.

What alternative did he have though? He was a scientist; it was his intellectual duty.

And in the meantime, the ephemeral show really was spectacular: the *Lampyridae* were flashing madly; the moths were swirling madly; the insectivorous bats and birds were having a ball; and the *stuff* escaping from its long and dismal confinement in the hollow of a dead pond, probably rendered far less than comfortable by the creeping effects of pesticide pollution, was presumably having a ball too: exuberance all round.

Hazard could not resist the temptation to join in. He vaulted over the wrought-iron gate, and made his way into the heart of the vast hive of fireflies, into the center of the light-show, raising his arms as if he were conducting that bizarre orchestra of pale luminescence. None of the others joined him; they were content to watch him play the part of a participant in the marvel, perhaps feeling that he was entitled, partly because it was his churchyard, and partly because he had been the vehicle that had released the stuff from the pond, but mostly because he was, after all, the entomologist. It was his prerogative.

And he danced. He couldn't fly, like the moths, but he could dance, to celebrate the beauty of the world, and all the history of life that had produced it.

The newly-metamorphosed beetles continued flashing for a long time—or so, at least, it seemed. Their display was, in its way, more exciting than any meteor shower or exceptional manifestation of the aurora borealis, especially if one could watch it, and participate in it, with a sophisticated understanding of its symbolism and significance.

As I can, Hazard thought, with a smug self-satisfaction the likes of which he hadn't felt for months: not since Jenny had left. *As I certainly can*.

XII

Hazard wasn't particularly surprised when Claire Croly's red Saxo made its way up the lane to the Old Vicarage six weeks later. She could have posted him a complimentary copy of the issue that contained her name-free account of the exotic haunting of Tenebrion Wood and the mysterious death of Adrian Stimpson, ecomartyr—but she was never going to do that now that she knew the way to where he lived. Hazard didn't invite her into the house, though. He was in the cemetery when she arrived, and it was among the tapestried gravestones—observed by wild bees, but with no *Lampyridae* or moths in evidence, it being not long after noon—that he received his gift. It was summer now, and the day was glorious. The overgrown graves were beautifully green, and the wild flowers that grew in profusion were as colorful a flock of alien species as any painter in Bedlam could have imagined.

"I can see why you like this place so much," the reporter said. "It must be at its best now."

"Pretty much," Hazard agreed, knowing that the young woman was hinting that it wasn't at its best at all just now. She had seen it at its best, and knew what its best really was, even if it had only attained it briefly, and might never attain it again.

"I've thought about writing an article about what we saw that night," she said. "I've tried, in fact, but I can't get a viable handle on it, story-wise. I know you explained it all, and I've tried to understand it. I think I do, except for the chemistry, but I can't make it plausible as a series of deductions, in such a way that our readers would be able to grasp it. It's too complicated."

"It *is* complicated," Hazard admitted, blandly. "Reality is like that. And it isn't plausible, in any way that your readers could digest. Reality is like that, too."

"You can be a patronizing bastard sometimes, can't you?" she said, but without any real venom or animosity. He supposed that they must know one another well enough by now to have a joking relationship of sorts.

"I try," he replied. He was joking too, but he suspected, on thinking about it, that he really did try, sometimes. It was one of the things that seemed to be expected of a university lecturer. It came with the image.

"You're still on your own, I suppose?" she asked, looking over at the house, although there was surely nothing about its appearance that betrayed the continued loneliness of his existence. "The little wife hasn't come back?"

"No," he admitted, curtly.

"But you still see a fair amount of Helen the biochemist?"

"A fair amount. We're working in association, but we mostly meet at the university to discuss findings and procedures. She doesn't visit me here—she doesn't own a car."

"And you're still in touch with the batty old lesbian?"

"She's not batty; she's exceedingly sane, and always intellectually stimulating company. We're still in touch. She takes an interest in our work. She doesn't have a car either, though."

"She and the postgrad aren't really an item, are they?"

"Not as far as I know. It's not something we discuss."

"No, of course not—you're an entomologist and she's a biochemist. No time for trivia, when the two of you are on the track of liquid life. After all, you don't need a wife or a girl-friend do you, when you have all of *this*." Her broad gesture indicated the churchyard, but was really intended to designate its insect life. She was still pretending to be joking.

"I could probably fit you into my schedule if you wanted to volunteer for the role," he said. "Even an entomologist has to make the effort to be a well-rounded human being."

"I've heard better chat-up lines," she told him, plausibly, "and I'd be bad for your image as a serious scientist. To be honest, though, you're not my type. Far too fond of beetles."

"As the great J. B. S. Haldane once said, when asked what a lifetime of study had taught him about the mind of the Creator, *it would appear that God has an inordinate fondness for beetles*, so I'm in the very best company there. Haldane was talking about the Christian God, of course, but the implication of Nature remains the same no matter how you animate it behind the scenes. My fondness isn't that unusual—remember the ancient Egyptians and fascination with their scarabs—and the affection is fully in tune with the world we live in. Can you be as confident about your affections?"

Her expression didn't give her the appearance of someone who could, but she wasn't about to be drawn into any kind of confession. "It's a pity your wife didn't feel the same," she said, instead.

"True," Hazard admitted. "But she couldn't help the way she felt. As I've explained to you before, the mind can play tricks when the senses are displaced into a new environment. Many things we've sub-consciously ceased to notice are suddenly conspicuous by their absence, and *vice versa*. Jenny thought living out in the country, next door to an old churchyard, would be romantic. She hadn't expected it to be scary, and she couldn't quite get her head around the notion that its seeming scariness was all in the eyes and ears of the beholder. She thought the place was haunted. She couldn't accept that the lights were just *Lampyridae*—to her, they really became lost souls, enigmatic night-spirits. She just couldn't shake the notion loose, even though she knew it wasn't true. It was simply too plausible. On the other hand, maybe Steve was right too—maybe, at an even deeper level, she just couldn't stand living with me any longer."

"He's right more often than one might think," Claire Croly told him. "He's right about your not being safe, even here. The day might well come when the Evil Developers' bulldozers appear, even on this remote horizon."

"Not in my lifetime," Hazard assured her. "There are no dominoes hereabouts of the kind he pointed out to me on his road map. Even if the farmer who owns the local fields weren't descended from a long line of agricultural geniuses, he'd never let go of his heritage the way the owner of Tenebrion Farm did. When it comes to stubbornness, he'd make even Steve look like a quivering mass of querulous capitulation. I've got the one and only hole in the patchwork. If there's a single safe residential dwelling within a hundred miles, this is it. The landscape's not natural, of course—everything the eye can see in every direction is the product of human artifice and the spirit of technological endeavor—but it's green, and it's alive. Every year it dies, and every year it comes back to life, al-ways changing, adapting, evolving. Especially the cemetery, where there really is life after death….and then some."

The reporter condescended to smile. Considering that he wasn't her type, and that he sometimes came across in her eyes as a patronizing bastard, she didn't seem to dislike him—or perhaps she simply thought that one day, she'd get a story out of him that she could actually use.

"It really wasn't haunted, back in the days when your wife ran away, was it?" she said.

"No," he replied, even though he knew exactly what she was going to say next, "it wasn't."

"But it is now," she said, fulfilling his private prophecy to the letter. "Isn't it?" She didn't mean that it was haunted by ghosts; she knew that the presence he'd imported from the late, lamented Tenebrion Wood was much more interesting night-spirit than that, at least to him.

"Oh yes," he said, serenely, and with satisfaction. "It is *now*."

CPSIA information can be obtained
at www.ICGtesting.com
Printed in the USA
LVOW12s1929090317
526680LV00004B/925/P

9 781479 421336